Chasing Normal

Also by Lisa Papademetriou:

Sixth-Grade Glommers, Norks, and Me

Chasing Normal

Lisa Papademetriou

Disney • Hyperion Books
New York

Text copyright © 2008 by Lisa Papademetriou

All rights reserved. Published by Disney • Hyperion Books, an imprint of Disney Book Group. No part of this book may be reproduced or transmitted in any form or by any means, electronic or mechanical, including photocopying, recording, or by any information storage and retrieval system, without written permission from the publisher. For information address Disney • Hyperion Books, 114 Fifth Avenue, New York, New York 10011-5690.

First Disney • Hyperion paperback edition, 2009
1 3 5 7 9 10 8 6 4 2
Library of Congress Cataloging-in-Publication Data on file.
ISBN: 978-1-4231-0341-7
Printed in the United States of America

Visit www.hyperionbooksforchildren.com

Acknowledgments

Many heartfelt thanks to Namrata Tripathi
and Helen Perelman for their encouragement
and insight.

For Marguerite Belkin

Chasing Normal

chapter one

I blinked up at the greenish star stickers on my bedroom ceiling as my heart beat a crazy drumbeat in my chest. The phone had just jangled me out of a particularly horrible algebra test nightmare, and it took me a minute to remember that it was July. No algebra. No pop quizzes. Not for another few weeks, anyway.

The phone rang twice more, and then I heard Dad's voice in the next room. I couldn't make out the words.

I rolled over and looked at the glowing digital numbers on the ancient clock radio beside my bed. Four in the morning? Wait—that couldn't be right. Nobody in their right mind would call Dad at four in the morning. Everyone knows he's useless before noon. And even weirder, Dad had answered it. After what seemed like a long time, I heard him hang up.

I was just debating whether or not to get out of bed when the hallway light clicked on and crept in under my door. Then there was a knock, and I heard my father's voice gently say, "Mieka?"

"I'm awake."

Dad pushed open my door and stood there for a moment, his dark eyes huge. That alone made me nervous, so I sat up straight. "What's wrong?"

You see, Dad doesn't actually open his eyes when he wakes up. He wanders around the apartment, his eyelids narrowed into tiny slits as he barely avoids bumping into one thing after another. Dad takes about an hour and a half plus three cups of coffee in order to reach a state that most people would call "awake."

On the flip, I'm a morning person. The moment my eyes snap open, I'm awake. Fully awake. There's no going back to bed. The wheels in my brain start spinning, and once that machine is rolling, I just have to give in. That's why I prefer to study for tests in the morning. I'll get up at five, shower, make the bed, and get to work. I'm like Nana that way.

"What's wrong?" I asked. "Did something happen?"

"Your grandmother—" Dad's voice was really strange, like it was coming from somewhere other than his body.

"Nana?" I whispered.

Dad shook his head. "No—Grandma Baker. She's in the hospital."

"Oh." It took me a moment to register my dad's words. Grandma Baker. *His* mother. I didn't know what to say.

Dad stepped into my room. The end of my mattress groaned as he sat down. "That was your aunt Kate on the phone. Grandma is very sick."

I nodded.

"Aunt Kate wants us to come to Houston," Dad went on.

"Houston?" I repeated.

"For a visit," Dad explained.

I thought about that. Grandma Baker. Aunt Kate. Houston, Texas. "For how long?" I asked.

"I don't know. A couple of weeks, I guess."

We stared at each other. In the dim light from the hall, I could see the lines at the edges of my father's eyes. His hair had gone gray right after Mom left—

it was a pretty silver color that reminded me of our toaster. The gray made him look older than most of my friends' dads. "Do you want to go?" I asked him.

"I'm not sure." Dad's fingers traced the swirly orange pattern on my quilt. "What do you think?"

"I don't know." I didn't, either. I'd only ever met Grandma Baker once, when I was five. I didn't remember it. She and my father were estranged. I didn't really know why. Just like I didn't know why my mother left us, why she lived in California now, why she wrote but never called. All I knew was that I had the World's Smallest Family—Dad, Nana, and the Christmas cards and cheery family newsletters from Aunt Kate's family.

Anyway, I wasn't too sure what to think about Grandma Baker. My other grandmother—Nana—lives five blocks from us in Boston, so we spend a lot of time together. She takes me shopping and loves to play board games and go to Jazzercise class, and she makes the best rugelach in the universe. Also, she owns this cool little vintage store called Rewind. I'm glad that she and my dad stayed close, even when Mom took off. Sometimes I like to look at the pictures of Mom in

Nana's apartment. She never put them away, but she never talks about them, either.

Dad's bottom lip crawled over his top, tucking it into a frown. He does that when he's thinking hard about something. I decided to do what I always do when I can't decide something—I sized up the facts. So here they are:

1. Dad hadn't spoken to Grandma Baker in seven years.

2. Aunt Kate wouldn't have called at four in the morning unless it was important.

3. It might be my last chance to get to know Grandma.

4. I hadn't seen Aunt Kate, Uncle Dave, Cousin Greta, or Cousin Mark in almost three years. Right after Mom moved, they came to Massachusetts and we all spent two weeks on Cape Cod. I remember splashing around in the waves with Greta, digging up tiny purple clams, and building drippy sand castles with shells for doors. Dad still has a picture taped to the refrigerator of me and Greta buried up to our necks in sand. We're smiling, like friends.

5. I knew from Aunt Kate's yearly newsletter that her house had a pool.

Suddenly, I saw three weeks of lounging by the clear blue water, drinking lemonade, and playing cards with Greta. I saw my father and Grandma making up and acting like a family again. I'd miss spending the end of summer at the park near our house, and I'd miss my room, and all of that. But my best friend, Tricky—I mean, Theresa—had already left for camp. Besides, she'd been acting kind of weird for the past few weeks. So—even if she were around—it wasn't like I'd be missing much.

"I think we should go," I said finally.

"Really?" Dad looked so surprised that it surprised me right back.

"Yeah—don't you?"

Dad sighed. "Yeah."

I put my hand on top of his, and his fingers stopped their crazy little quilt-tracing dance. "It'll be fun," I told him.

Dad's mouth moved, almost like he was going to smile—but the smile never actually showed up. "Okay," he said finally. He hauled himself off my mattress.

And just like that, everything changed.

"Mieka," Dad said as we walked through the Houston airport—the clean, clean airport. It was cleaner than a hospital. We'd just touched down, and I felt like I'd stepped out of the airplane and onto another planet.

"Yeah?" I asked as I gave my wheeled luggage a yank. Roll straight, I commanded silently, but the bag ignored me. It flopped over, like it was exhausted from all of the traveling it had done, and I had to kick at it to get it going again.

"Would you just . . ." Dad stared straight ahead, and his voice trailed off.

"What?"

Dad shook his head. Then he tried again. "Would you just—try to—"

"Try to what?" I peered in the window of the Body Shop. Jeez, this airport was the nicest mall I'd ever been in.

"Just be on your best behavior, okay?" Dad looked nervous, like he expected the ceiling to cave in, or something.

"Of course," I told him. Then I thought about that for a minute. "Wait—what are you afraid I'm going to do?"

Dad blew out a sigh. "I have no idea," he admitted. "Let's just both be on our best behavior, all right?"

I didn't have time to answer, though, because just then we walked out of the terminal and I got smacked in the face by a solid mass of heat. I'm not kidding. It was like walking straight into a mound of Jell-O, or something. The air was *thick*.

Dad looked around, then waved quickly. I followed his gaze. There they were. The living embodiment of the Christmas card we received every year. Only they weren't wearing red-and-black plaid.

"Jeffrey!" Aunt Kate bobbed on the balls of her feet as we made our way toward her. She was tall, with short blond hair and my dad's long nose. "Jeff! Over here!"

"Uncle Jeff!" Cousin Greta gave him a huge smile and waved. I was amazed at how much she and Aunt Kate looked alike, given the fact that they didn't look alike at all. It was more that they moved in the same way. And they had the same smile.

My stomach sank. Greta reminded me of Arielle McPherson, this witchy girl who rides my bus. Both were really pretty—blue eyes, blond hair, perfect teeth. And both managed to look superclean. Groomed, that's the word. I don't know why, but my clothes are always kind of rumpled and messy. But her pink tank top and khaki shorts looked brand new. I tugged at my shoulder-length brown hair, trying to remember if I'd brushed it or not. The tangles that caught at my fingers said *nope*.

"Say hello to your uncle Jeffrey." Aunt Kate poked my other cousin, Mark, in the shoulder. He's the one that the yearly Christmas card always claims is a genius. He looked like a regular six-year-old to me.

"Ouch," Mark complained. He looked at me suspiciously from beneath his dark lashes, as though I was the one who had poked him.

"Hey, everyone," I said.

Dad leaned over and kissed his sister on the cheek. "Hi, Kate. Greta!" His eyes shone. "You're such a beautiful young lady!"

"Thank you," Greta said, like she'd heard that about a zillion times before.

My stomach sank even further, like it was on an escalator leading to my feet. Why doesn't Dad ever say anything like that to me? I wondered.

My aunt blushed a little. "Mieka, you're so grown up," she said.

I shrugged. "I'm twelve."

"Me too—I'll be twelve in December," Greta announced.

"Congratulations. That's only six months away," I told her. I took a deep breath and nearly choked on the fumes. There was something about this Houston air. It was almost like you needed a spoon to breathe it.

I was about to ask if it was always this hot, when someone honked. I stopped myself from shouting, "We can hear you, jerk!" which turned out to be a good thing, because the guy behind the wheel was Uncle Dave.

"Jeff-O!" he called. "Toss the bags in the back of the car and let's get out of here."

"Sure thing!" Dad said, only it sounded like "shar thang." Did he have a Texan accent five minutes ago? I wondered. Because I could have sworn he had one now.

"I'm sitting in the back, next to Mieka!" Greta called, taking my hand. I was a little embarrassed for her for sounding five years old. I was even more embarrassed for myself for feeling so happy and relieved that she wanted to sit next to me. She isn't Arielle, I told myself. She's your cousin—remember?

We scrambled into the car, which was sort of like climbing a mountain. Really, it was the biggest car I'd ever been in, and it had a weird smell that stuck to the inside of my nose.

"New car," Dad said, running his hand across the soft, tan leather seat.

"I needed a toy." Uncle Dave winked at my father in the rearview mirror. "Well there, Mieka, you sure do look like a young lady!"

"Thanks," I said, but what I thought was, Not a *beautiful* young lady?

"I hope you're ready to spend some time in our pool," Uncle Dave said. "Who wants to go swimming?"

"We do!" Greta and Mark screeched.

"Sweetheart, don't you think we should stop by the hospital first?" Aunt Kate suggested.

Dad leaned forward. "Yes, I'd—"

"Oh, they don't want to go rushing over to the hospital," Uncle Dave said. "Plenty of time for that. Let them get settled first."

"You'll be staying in my room," Greta told me.

I shrugged. "Okay," I said.

"Really, Dave." My father ran a hand through his gray hair. "I'd like to go to the—"

"I'll take you over there after lunch," Uncle Dave promised. "Unless we're having too much fun, right kids?"

Greta and Mark chorused their yeses as I leaned back against the leather seat and let the cool air-conditioning wash over me. Dad mashed his lips together and didn't say anything more. That was the thing about this Texas heat—even three minutes of it made you too tired to argue.

chapter two

"*D*o you want to check your e-mail, or something?" Greta asked as she pecked away at the computer keyboard. She had already changed into a pink tankini and was waiting for me to dig my bathing suit out of the bottom of my bag. The pink flip-flop on her right foot flapped impatiently against her heel as she peered at the screen. The keyboard pecking and the pink swimsuit made her look a little like a flamingo.

"No thanks," I told her. I was too embarrassed to tell her that I hardly ever check my e-mail since nobody ever writes me.

I pulled a sloppy pile of shorts and seven pairs of socks from my bag, placing them on the bed. Where did that stupid swimsuit go? I wondered as I yanked out my bright green nightshirt. Greta giggled and pressed SEND. She was chatting online with a couple of her friends.

"What's so funny?" I asked.

"Oh, nothing," Greta said, fidgeting in her plush blue chair. "Kristin just said something about this girl we know. She's got this weird way of talking—she kind of . . . spits on everyone." Greta winced. "I mean, she's really nice and everything—" Greta added quickly, "but you kind of have to wear a raincoat around her." She gave me a nervous look.

"I'll bring a plastic bag to wear on my hair," I said.

"Do you think I'm hideously mean?" Greta asked.

I think you sound like Arielle McPherson, I thought, but what I said was, "Of course not."

Smiling, Greta turned back to the computer as I put my green nightshirt on the pile of purple pillows on my bed. *My* bed—I was still getting used to the concept. At home, I've got a mattress on the floor. It's really comfortable, and I like feeling like I'm in a little nest. But Greta had twin beds, and they even had headboards and footboards. They were wood and painted white to go with the white bureau on the far wall near the d[...]

Greta's room was just about the prettiest place I'd ever been. Everything in the room was blue, purple, or white. Even the ceiling was blue, and had clouds painted on it. Aunt Kate had painted the clouds, just like she'd painted the stars and planets in Mark's room. She was a terrific painter, which shouldn't have surprised me as much as it did. Art must run in the family.

Finally, my silky, navy blue one-piece appeared stuffed into the corner beneath my underwear. I held it up, noticing for the first time that the elastic at the neck was starting to fray.

Greta laughed again and pecked at the keyboard some more. I felt a hot stab of envy. I couldn't help it—her room, her computer, her beautiful non-frizzy blond hair, her pink tankini—everything about her was perfect. I pictured myself standing beside her, with Aunt Kate, Uncle Dave, and Cousin Mark. Me in my falling-apart swimsuit and pink high-tops. I didn't quite belong—like a toad at a tea party. "Is Kristin your best friend?" I asked suddenly.

Greta looked at me with those blue blue blue eyes—the same color as the sky on her ceiling. "Yeah," she said, then hesitated. "Yeah," she said again. "Kristin and Julie and I are all best friends."

Of course perfect Greta had a best friend—and not just one, but two. I thought about Tricky—how we used to be BFFs. Until Arielle came along. Until they decided I was weird.

Greta's cheeks flushed slightly pink, and she turned back to her computer. "I'll be off in a minute," she said. "Then we can go down to the pool."

A splash told me that someone—probably Uncle Dave, judging by the noise—had beaten us to it. I balled up my bathing suit and headed toward the door so I could change in the bathroom down the hall. "I'll be ready," I said.

"Marco!" Mark shouted.

"Polo!" the rest of us cried. I stayed very still while Greta sloshed away from him at top speed. Naturally, Mark dove after the sound of her splashes.

She shrieked as he grabbed her arm.

"I got you!" he shouted, flipping a chunk of wet hair out of his eyes.

"You're cheating!" she cried.

Laughing, Uncle Dave splashed Mark, then the two kids piled onto him and dunked him. I floated on my back for a minute. "I'm getting kind of thirsty," I said to no one in particular just as Uncle Dave surfaced, whalelike, and splashed me, too.

"Get her!" Mark cried.

Greta sent a tsunami my way, so I exhaled and sank to the bottom of the pool. I really hate getting splashed. I know, I know—I was in the pool, I was already wet, what's the big deal? I have no idea. I just don't like it. I swam like a dolphin to the gleaming metal ladder and hauled myself out.

I hurried over to where Aunt Kate was sitting in the shade of a table umbrella. Mark sent a few more strategic splashes my way, but Uncle Dave squirted him and told him to cut it out.

"Is there any more lemonade?" I asked Aunt Kate as I stood on the hot concrete, my feet burning while the rest of me dripped, drying fast in the sun. She was wearing enormous sunglasses and a wide-brimmed straw hat.

Aunt Kate looked up from her book. "There's plenty in the fridge," she said, starting to stand up.

"Meeks can help herself," my dad said. He was sitting on a lounge chair with a magazine in his lap. He didn't really seem to be reading it, though. I hadn't seen him turn a page in twenty minutes.

Aunt Kate hesitated, then looked up at me. I couldn't read her expression through her dark glasses, but finally she said, "All right."

I grabbed my glass from the table. It was empty, except for a dreary puddle at the bottom, where my ice cubes had melted. The sun beat down on my scalp, turning my dark hair hot. The sky was bluer than blue, and some insects were making a shirring sound, like gears grinding in a car, or like a kitchen appliance on the blink.

A chill shivered over my body as I walked in through the sliding-glass door. The air-conditioning cooled the droplets on my skin, raising goose bumps on my arms, as I walked up to the giant, beautiful, stainless steel refrigerator.

Here is the thing about Aunt Kate's house—it's perfect. My dad gets these catalogs for furniture and home stuff, and Aunt Kate's house looks just like that. Each room is a different page. I half-expected to see the letter *G* dangling beside the coffee table, along with a description of where it was made and the price.

"We have our own unique style" is what my dad is always saying about our house. Unique is pretty accurate, I'd say. All of our furniture is from Nana's store, Rewind. Nana refers to the stuff in the store as "mid-twentieth-century modern artifacts," but I think most people would call it a "thrift store." But it's a specific thrift store—everything in it is from the 1950s and 60s. Which means that our house is a major time warp.

"Your living room looks like the inside of a spaceship," my friend Tricky said the first time she walked into our apartment. It's kind of true. We have these white chairs that look like pods on sticks and this crazy orange shag carpet. We have a white telephone shaped like a banana. The numbers are on the bottom of the phone. Our coffee table is a white oval. And then there are the walls, which are covered in Dad's crazy art. I like our place, but everyone who walks in has a comment. Or comments.

It would be so much easier to have a place like this, I thought as I looked around my aunt's home. The kitchen was superclean—all of the steel appliances gleaming. And it was new. Brand new. Our fridge doesn't even have an ice maker, I thought as I switched the setting on the door to "crushed ice" and pressed my glass against the lever. Ice magically clinked into the glass. I filled it two-thirds of the way.

I yanked open the door and a cloud of mist spilled out. More cool air blasted me, and my teeth actually chattered a bit. This is the most organized refrigerator I've ever seen, I thought. At home, everything is just shoved in any which way. But here, all of the sodas and drinks were arranged neatly in the lower left corner. There were labeled drawers. "Greens," one read. "Root Vegetables," read another. I pulled open the one marked, "Kid Snacks," and was greeted with an arrangement of string cheese, peanut-butter crackers, and granola bars. I wasn't hungry, but I grabbed a granola bar, anyway. Just because I could. Then I filled my glass with lemonade from the tall glass pitcher on the bottom left shelf and closed the door.

Through the glass door, I watched as Mark scrambled out of the pool and jumped back in, blasting a cannonball all over Uncle Dave and Greta. I decided to poke around the house.

The living room was gorgeous and four times the size of ours—but it looked like nobody ever used it. An arched ceiling towered above me, making me dizzy. Light streamed in from the windows that reached almost to the top. How do they clean them? I wondered. The couches were cream colored and uncomfortable looking and arranged facing each other in front of a stone fireplace. A fireplace! I had to wonder how often they put a log in there. I mean, if it was about a thousand degrees outside now, would it cool off to just a hundred by Christmas?

Weirdest of all, there wasn't any stuff in this room. I mean, there were chairs and pillows and a nice coffee table, but there wasn't any *junk*. No paperbacks tossed aside, no shoes, no half-empty cups lingering on a table, no random bicycle pump that someone forgot to put away, no mail—none of the stuff that we always seem to have all over the place.

Aunt Kate had given us a tour of the house when we first got here, but I still felt like exploring. I really wanted to see the guest room again. That was where Grandma would be staying when she got home from the hospital. It was like a real room, with a huge bed and a dresser and everything. It was nicer than Dad's bedroom at home. And most of the time nobody even lived there!

Grandma had her own apartment about a mile away, but she wasn't going back there—not yet, anyway. Aunt Kate insisted that she needed someone to take care of her. She needed her family around. I could understand that.

I walked through a door into the room where my dad was going to be sleeping on the fold-out couch—the family room. The couch was sage green and over-stuffed, squishy and comfy. The far wall held a huge flat-panel TV next to a bunch of shelves piled with games. My dad's dingy suitcase and backpack lay huddled in a corner—the only flaw in the place. This whole room is just for fun, I thought as I looked around. Peering at the shelves, I saw that they had every game I had ever heard of, and a few I hadn't. There was backgammon, chess, checkers, five decks of cards, Monopoly, Risk, Cranium, three shelves full of puzzle boxes, Operation, Sorry, Life, Trivial Pursuit, Hoopla—

"Do you want to play something?"

I jumped at the voice. "Jeez, Mark," I said, whipping

around to face him, "you shouldn't sneak up on people like that."

Mark shrugged. "Sorry." He was dripping wet—he hadn't even grabbed a towel. Now he was tracking water everywhere. Man, if I had a house this nice, I'd wipe my feet before I stepped inside, I thought. But I guessed that Mark was just used to it. He eyed the granola bar in my hand, and I felt a flash of hot flame shoot across my cheeks. "I was hungry," I said quickly.

"So am I." Mark nodded. "Can I have some?"

I plucked off part of the granola bar, feeling suddenly bad for taking it without asking. "Is it okay?" I asked as I handed him a chunk.

"What?" He popped the piece into his mouth and chewed.

"The granola bar," I explained. "Can I have it?"

Mark shrugged. "Why not?"

"Mieka!" a voice singsonged.

"Greta's looking for you," Mark said. Unnecessarily, I might add. "I think she wants to race you from one end of the pool to the other."

I wanted to keep exploring, but I didn't want to be rude. Who knew how long Dad and I would be here?

I'm sure I'll have plenty of time to see everything, I told myself. "Let's go."

Mark's wet feet slapped against the floor as he raced toward the back door. I had to force myself not to use my towel to dry up his footprints.

He didn't have any idea how perfect his house—his life—was.

chapter three

"*I*s that what you're wearing to see Grandma?" Greta asked me later as I was buttoning up a bowling shirt. It was my favorite shirt—black, with tiny white bowling pins for buttons. It read BOWLTOWN LANES across the back, and the name over the pocket on the front was "Earl." I found it on the rack at Nana's, of course. Earl must have been a small guy, because the shirt was big on me, but not freakishly huge, just roomy.

There's something great about the way soft fabric feels against your skin after you've been swimming— when you're clean and dry. My old shirt and my khaki shorts had been feeling wonderful right up to the moment when Greta asked me that question.

"Yeah," I said as I eyed the green sundress Greta had just pulled on. It was perfectly ironed. I couldn't remember the last time I'd worn a dress. Suddenly, I felt like I should be wearing something nicer. But I hadn't brought anything. Not that I'd had much to choose from in the first place. I looked down at my wrinkled outfit. "Do you think it's okay?"

"Sure," Greta said, but her face said the opposite.

My friend Tricky used to say that I was "fashion impaired." It never really bothered me until the end of this year, when she started hanging out with Arielle McPherson. Then they both started saying it.

That bothered me.

"Girls, are you ready?" Aunt Kate asked from the other side of the door. She poked her head inside, and her sunny smile evaporated. "Mieka honey, is that what you're wearing?" she asked me.

"Yes," I told her. I wanted to add, "Sorry," but knew it would sound weird, so I just kept quiet.

"Oh." Aunt Kate smiled again. "Okay. So I guess we're all ready."

We stepped into the hall just as Mark walked out of his room wearing khakis and a polo shirt. He gaped at me, and then glared at his mother. "How come Mieka gets to wear shorts?" he demanded.

"Mieka hasn't seen Grandma in a long time," Aunt Kate replied, smoothing a nonexistent wrinkle in her melon-colored capri pants. "Grandma isn't going to care about her clothes."

Mark gave his mom a look I couldn't figure out, and then Uncle Dave shouted at us from downstairs to get a move on, so we hurried down the steps and piled into the SUV, where my father was already sitting shotgun. His gray hair looked unusually tidy, like he'd raked a comb through it, but he was wearing his usual crumpled shirt and shorts, so I didn't feel so bad. At least I wasn't the only wrinkled one.

Uncle Dave's cell phone rang the minute we pulled up to the hospital. "I've got to take this," he said, glancing at the number.

"You're not coming up?" Aunt Kate asked.

"I'll be up as soon as I'm off the call," Uncle Dave replied; he settled an earpiece into his ear and said, "This is Dave Williston."

"Come on, kids." Yanking open his car door, Dad stepped onto the curb, so we all piled out after him.

Even the thirty-second walk from the car to the hospital lobby was enough for the heat to settle over my skin like a hot, wet blanket. I had never been so grateful for air-conditioning in my life.

We squeaked down the hall and then filed into an elevator. Nobody said anything as the doors closed and we started moving up, up, up, but I felt my stomach drop and my heart give a flutter. I'm going to see Grandma Baker, I thought. I felt dizzy and nervous and excited, all swirled together like a tropical storm.

I wonder if Dad will cry when he sees Grandma, I thought when the elevator doors opened again. I hoped not. It's weird to see your parents cry. But it would be okay if she cries when she sees us, I decided.

Once we reached the end of the hall, Aunt Kate knocked softly on the door. "Hi, Mom!" she sang as she swung it open. "We brought you some visitors."

A huge woman with short gray hair was lying propped up in a hospital gown, the television clicker in her hand. "This cheap hospital you stuck me in only gives you basic cable," she griped. Then her steely blue eyes took in the scene at the doorway. If she seemed surprised to see her son, she didn't show it.

"Hi, Ma," my dad said. His voice was soft. It reminded me of the time he had shown me a nest full of baby birds in the big maple at the end of our street. There were three of them, all beak and wrinkled skin as they held their mouths open in the hope of getting something to eat. "Don't startle them," he'd whispered then.

My heart felt like it was swelling, like it might burst.

For a moment, nobody spoke. Nobody moved. The television blared on, trying to sell us some toothpaste that would change our lives.

Grandma's mouth twisted. "So you finally decided to show up," she said at last. "I guess I must really be sick." She turned her attention back to the television set and changed the channel.

I peeked over at my dad, who looked like someone had just slapped him.

"Mom, this is Mieka," Aunt Kate said, putting her hands on my shoulders. "Jeff's daughter. Remember?"

This was enough to make Grandma turn off the television set, although she didn't let go of the remote. Her blue eyes sent a cold chill over me as she gave me an up-and-down look. "You got big," she said.

"You haven't seen Mieka since she was five," my father said. "She grew up."

"She gained some weight is what she did," Grandma shot back.

Now I felt like *I'd* been slapped—my own grandmother had just called me *fat*.

"Mieka just has on a roomy shirt," Dad said.

"Hm." Grandma sounded like she didn't believe it. And she gave me a look that said she didn't think much of my shirt, either. "Why is everyone standing around like lumps?" Grandma Baker demanded. "Don't you kids want to give your grandma a kiss?"

Mark shuffled over after Greta, who had hurried to give Grandma a kiss on the cheek. He leaned in and kissed Grandma like he was kissing a snake. She gave him a steady look. "You need a breath mint," she told my cousin.

Aunt Kate winced as Mark glowered at our grandmother.

"Mom." My dad sounded shocked, but not shocked at the same time. He shook his head.

"I'm just being helpful," she snapped. "This family needs some help. You should get an iron," she added to my father. "Your daughter looks like she just stepped out of the bottom of the hamper."

Warm tears sprang up in my eyes and my throat felt thick, like there was something stuck in it. Don't cry in front of her, I commanded myself. Do not cry.

I felt my father's warm hand slip around mine. "Look, Ma, we can't stay long," Dad said.

"You never do," Grandma shot back. She turned her glance to my aunt. "Don't worry—hospitals are full of people who don't get any visitors. I'm not the only one."

"We were here just yesterday," Aunt Kate pointed out.

Grandma just snorted and clicked the TV back on.

"We'll come back when you're feeling better," my dad told her, but she didn't even look in his direction.

I held in the tears as we walked down the long white hall. They didn't spill out until we were at the elevator. My father leaned against the wall, obviously miserable, and it was Greta who patted my shoulder. "Don't worry," she said. "That's just how she is."

I nodded, but I still couldn't stop crying. It was easy for her to say—Grandma hadn't called *her* fat. Greta put an arm around me. I had a momentary impulse to shrug it off, and then felt an immediate pang of guilt. Greta was just trying to be nice. It wasn't her fault that she looked perfect and I was a big, chunky wrinkle-ball. I let her keep her arm around me until we reached the lobby.

Uncle Dave was still on the phone when we reached the car. It seemed like he wasn't going to get off, either, until he saw my face. The minute he did, he said, "Jim, I'm going through a tunnel. I'm going to have to call you back," and then he turned to me and said, "What happened to you?"

"Grandma said something mean," Mark snapped. He didn't say "again," but it sounded like that's what he meant.

"Mark," Aunt Kate said in a warning tone.

"I'm just explaining why Mieka's crying," Mark said, folding his arms across his chest and digging into his seat in the back corner of the SUV.

"It's okay," I said kind of shakily. Everyone was staring at me. I felt like a matchstick—like my face might burst into flames. "I'm okay."

Uncle Dave chuckled. "Well, she's a real character,

that one," he said, yanking the car into reverse and steering out of the parking spot. "You never know what Mama Baker's going to say, that much is for sure. Am I right, Jeff-O, or am I right?"

In the passenger seat, my father leaned the side of his forehead against the window. "You're right," he said at last.

Aunt Kate sat tight-lipped behind her brother.

"Okay, kids," Uncle Dave said cheerfully, "who wants ice cream?"

"Me," Mark howled.

"I do," Greta said softly. She gave my elbow a gentle nudge. I couldn't help thinking about how my grandmother had said I was fat. I'm not, I thought. I mean, I'm not a pole, like Greta. But I'm not overweight. I have boobs, though. They appeared suddenly at the end of last year. I didn't really even notice them until one day on the bus Arielle said, "Hey, Mieka, when are you going to get a bra?" really loudly. Everyone cracked up in this snorty way—like they were trying not to—and that's when I realized that my body was different than it had been. I wasn't stick-straight any more.

Having someone call you fat is a great way to make ice cream seem unappealing. Still, Greta was looking at me eagerly, and I could feel Mark staring at the back of my head.

"Someone didn't answer my ques-tion," Uncle Dave singsonged. "I said, 'Who wants ice cream?'"

"We do," Greta and Mark replied. This time, I joined them.

"What *is* that?" Greta asked as I dug my spoon into the pink-and-green ice cream. I had just spat out a green chunk and put it on my napkin. It looked a little like a piece of kryptonite.

"Bubble gum with marshmallow sauce," I told her. "I'm saving the gum for last."

Greta looked horrified, which made me laugh. It *was* kind of gross, I had to admit. "I can't chew gum and eat ice cream at the same time," I explained.

Greta looked down at her dish of chocolate. "Why get bubble gum ice cream in the first place? I didn't even know they made that flavor."

"It sounds great!" Mark chimed in from across the table.

Greta rolled her eyes. Mark was eating a flavor called "grasshopper," so his opinion didn't really count for much.

"I made a bet with Dad at the beginning of the summer," I explained.

"Mieka always gets strawberry," Dad said, taking a lick of his mocha ice-cream cone. "I was sick of watching her eat that pink ice cream."

I shrugged. "I like what I like."

"I'm the same way," Aunt Kate said. "For me, it's maple walnut or nothing."

Uncle Dave just shook his head. He had a big bowl with three different flavors in it.

"But she refused to even *try* something new," Dad said. "How can you be sure that strawberry is your favorite when there's a whole world of stuff you've never tried?"

"So Dad bet that I couldn't go the whole summer without eating the same flavor twice." I took another spoonful of my bubble gum flavor. As much as I hated to admit it—it was surprisingly good with the marshmallow. Not better than strawberry, but good.

"That's really weird," Greta said.

"What do you get if you do it?" Mark wanted to know.

"A skateboard," I told him.

Mark's eyes went round. He was impressed, I could tell. Greta had no comment.

"Well, this is the right place for you, then," Uncle Dave said.

"Dip has new flavors every day." Aunt Kate gestured toward the board where the special flavors were written in colorful chalk. They even had jalapeño flavor. I wondered what Greta would have thought if I'd ordered that.

"Hey, Greta," said a soft voice. A pretty girl with dark red hair stopped at our table.

"Emma!" Greta hopped up, wrapping the girl in a hug. "How's your summer?"

"Good—yours?"

"Oh, you know." Greta shrugged in a way that could have meant anything. Then she waved her hand in our general direction. "This is my family." I waited for her to introduce me. She didn't.

Emma smiled shyly. "Hi," she said, waving with just her fingers. Her eyes stopped at the table, and she got this weird look on her face. I felt myself blush—she was gaping at my napkin full of discarded bubble gum pieces.

But Emma didn't say anything like "Eww" or "Yuck" or "Greta, how can you be related to such a slob?" She just said, "Well, I'm here with—" and motioned to an athletic-looking couple that was sitting at a booth near the back. They each had a pair of sunglasses perched on top of their heads. The woman had dark red hair—Emma's parents, obviously.

"Cool," Greta said.

"Okay, well, I'll see you around?" Emma asked.

"Definitely!" Greta gave her another little hug, and after casting one last confused glance at my napkin, Emma hurried off to join her parents.

"Who was that, sweetie?" Aunt Kate asked as Greta slipped back into her seat.

Greta lifted one shoulder. "Just some girl from school."

"You don't even know her?" I asked.

"Not really." Greta took another spoonful of ice cream. "She's a year ahead of me."

Wow. I was amazed at how confident Greta was. She gave that Emma girl a hug and everything. And she didn't even know her! If I did that at school, people would think I was seriously off. But there was something about Greta. The Discovery Channel should make a documentary about her, I thought. *Perfection: One Girl's Story*.

Aunt Kate cleared her throat. "So, Jeff," she said brightly, "any ideas what you'd like to do while you're here?"

A look of confusion flickered across Dad's face. "Well—we're just here to see Mom," he said.

"Seeing Mama Baker's not going to take all day every day for three weeks," Uncle Dave pointed out.

That was the truth. Time didn't exactly fly by with Grandma around.

"I don't know . . . maybe we could see the sights." Dad sounded vague, like he hadn't thought about it much.

"Well." Aunt Kate stuck her spoon into her small blob of ice cream and took a sip of water. Then she dabbed at her lips with a paper napkin, placed that neatly on the table, folded her hands, and said, "Greta and Mark have activities during the day."

"They do?" I asked, starting to worry. Wait—am I

going to have to sit around by myself all day? I wondered.

"Mark goes to a learning academy and Greta goes to Camp Franklin," Aunt Kate said. She was looking at my father, not at me.

"Camp Franklin," he repeated. Like he knew what it was.

"And I think that maybe Mieka should go, too," Aunt Kate announced. "I think it's the only thing that makes sense—otherwise you'll be stuck at home all day, bored." She had picked up the napkin and was twisting it in her hands, wringing its neck, almost.

"I've never been to camp," I said.

"It's just day camp," Greta said. "It's like school."

"It's not like school." Aunt Kate sounded kind of insulted at the idea.

Greta shrugged. "It's like school with canoes and archery. And songs about Jesus."

"What?" I paused with my spoon halfway to my lips.

"That's the part I'm uncomfortable with," my dad said, running a hand through his silver hair.

"It's technically an Episcopal camp," Aunt Kate explained. "But it's just like regular camp."

Except for the songs about Jesus, I thought, but decided not to say. Not that I have anything against Jesus. I just don't know that much about him. Except that his face occasionally appears on the random potato chip.

Dad sighed. "I don't know," he said.

"It's a good place," Uncle Dave said heartily. "Good staff—well run. Loads of activities. Lots of the neighborhood kids go there. Even non-Episcopalians."

Aunt Kate wrapped her snakelike napkin around her index finger. "Jeff, I know you're not really interested in church . . ." Her voice trailed off.

Saying that my dad is "not really interested in church" is like saying chocolate is "kinda delicious." I've never even been inside a church, except the one time I slept over at Tricky/Theresa's house, and her family took me to Catholic Mass. Tricky said it was a "folk Mass," which meant that there were two people with guitars. We sang a bunch of songs and we all ate bagels afterward. It was nice.

Dad sat back against the booth. "Do they still have the orange doughnut?" he asked at last.

"Yeah!" Greta giggled. "They just had to get a new one!"

Orange doughnut? "Wait a minute—" I said slowly as a new idea dawned on me, "did *you* go there?"

Dad looked at Aunt Kate. "We both did," he said.

"It's changed," Aunt Kate told him. "But not much."

A smile passed between them, and I remembered that they were brother and sister. I mean, I *knew* that, of course. But I'd never really pictured them as kids before.

"I think that Mieka will like it," Aunt Kate said gently. "Greta loves it. Don't you, sweetie?"

"It's fun," Greta said.

"I want to try it," I said to my dad, thinking about how cool it would be to see the place where he went to camp.

Dad's eyebrows crept together. "Really?"

"Yeah!" Greta wrapped me in a hug, squeezing the air out of me. "You have to come!"

"I have to come," I repeated. "Greta says so."

"You don't have to do what she says," Mark pointed out.

"She can't just sit at home by herself," Aunt Kate prompted. "And the girls will be home by two thirty."

Dad heaved another sigh. "Okay," he said at last.

"All right!" Greta held up her hand, and I gave her a high five.

I didn't really know what to think of camp, but I sure liked the sound of that orange doughnut.

chapter four

Wednesday morning Aunt Kate whipped up some blueberry pancakes while Dad made berry smoothies in the blender. We'd spent the first part of the week "on vacation," as Dad put it, which meant sleeping in and eating huge breakfasts.

"Do you want to go to the Galleria later?" Greta asked as she speared a blueberry with her fork and twisted it out of the pancake. Greta's pancakes looked like crumbly Swiss cheese.

"What's that?" I drained the last of the smoothie from my glass. All that was left was a rim of pink scum and a few sad little raspberry seeds at the bottom.

"It's a dumb shopping mall," Mark said.

"It's not dumb," Greta shot back.

"What'll we do there?" I asked. It didn't surprise me that Greta wanted to go shopping. She was the type.

"I don't know." Greta shrugged. "Walk around. See a movie, maybe? They have an ice-skating rink."

"It's July," I pointed out.

"It's an indoor skating rink," Aunt Kate put in.

Whoa. Houston is a really interesting place. It's hot like crazy, but people here have figured out how to deal with it—mostly by never going outside. For one thing, everything is a drive-through. Dry cleaning, banking, shoe repair, you name it, you never have to get out of your car. And now an indoor ice-skating rink. I wanted to go just to see it. "Okay."

"I'll come with you girls," Aunt Kate said. "There are a few things I wanted to pick up."

"What about me?" Mark asked.

"You can come with us, chief," Uncle Dave said. He was supposedly taking the week off from work, even though he seemed to spend most of his time on his cell phone or dashing into the office to "straighten something out." "Your uncle Jeff and I are going to play racquetball at the health club."

Mark looked at his mother in horror.

"You're going over to Carl's house this afternoon, remember?" she said, and relief flooded Mark's face.

I wished that Uncle Dave had invited *me* to play racquetball. It sounded more fun than walking around the Galleria.

At least we weren't going to see Grandma.

Greta wanted to show me the ice rink right away, but Aunt Kate insisted that we walk through Macy's department store with her. "You need to get a few things for camp next week," she told Greta as she steered us into the juniors section.

Loud music blared from television screens posted at the corners of the juniors section, and brightly colored tops and shorts were hanging everywhere. Imagine being on the set of a music video directed by Willy Wonka, if he'd been really into clothes instead of candy. Dad and I don't usually do our shopping at department stores. More like outlet places, or Target, or even "Salvation Armani," as my dad calls the Salvation Army. Or Nana's shop, of course.

As Aunt Kate led Greta to a table of neatly folded

T-shirts, I toyed with a yellow dress hanging on a rack at the edge of the candy clothing section. It was pretty, and made of T-shirt material, so it looked comfortable.

"Would y'all like a dressing room?" drawled a tall African American woman with purplish hair the color of liver.

"Just browsing," I said automatically. It's what Nana always says when we're out window-shopping.

"Mieka honey, do you like that dress?" Aunt Kate appeared from nowhere, holding an armful of thick cotton T-shirts.

"Oooh, I love it," Greta said, barging through the racks to touch the fabric.

"You need something for church," Aunt Kate went on. "Why don't you try it on?"

"Church? I don't—" I couldn't make myself say that I didn't have any money.

But Aunt Kate just nodded encouragingly. "I'll get it for you, sweetie."

"I don't know," I mumbled. For some reason, I had this feeling that Dad wouldn't like it if he knew that Aunt Kate was buying me stuff, although I couldn't figure out why. Dad loves a bargain, and he loves getting stuff for free. In fact, he always says that our family motto is: "If free, take." Besides, Aunt Kate is family. If she wanted to get me a present, why shouldn't she?

Aunt Kate shot the saleslady a look that said, Grab the dress. "What size?" she asked me.

I winced, and peeked over at Greta. She had wandered over to a nearby rack to examine some jeans. The legs were the width of one of those cardboard rolls at the center of toilet paper. What size is that? I wondered. Do they make negative sizes? "I . . . I'm not sure," I lied.

"Hey, Mom?" Greta held up the teeny-tiny jeans. "Can I try these?"

"Sweetie, don't you have enough jeans?" Aunt Kate asked. "What about those green capris?" My aunt wandered over for a pants consultation, leaving me alone with the saleslady.

I flipped through the dresses and pulled out one in my size. "I think this will fit," I said as I handed it to the saleslady.

She blinked her big eyes slowly, and then nodded, "I'll start a dressing room for you."

Aunt Kate and Greta strolled through the department pulling out shorts and tops for me to try. I felt like I was on one of those makeover shows.

I stopped at a pair of denim shorts. They had embroidered flowers at the pockets—red poppies.

Aunt Kate caught me. "Those are adorable! Get a pair."

I flipped over the price tag. Ouch. I'd never even *heard* of shorts costing this much. "Um . . . I don't know. . . ."

But my aunt reached out and grabbed the shorts. "Just try them," she said. "If they look cute, we'll get them." Then she bustled off to where Greta was looking over some sleeveless button-down shirts.

I followed in a daze. I've never, never been able to walk into a store and just buy whatever I wanted. Never. And I mean I've never been able to do that at an *inexpensive* store. This shopping-explosion department store, with its sweet smells and bright lights and expensive clothes, was like another planet.

I looked down at my jeans. Secondhand from Salvation Armani. They were brand new when I got them; still had the tags on. What a find—new Levis in my size. They were a serious score. Last year, before her dad got a new job, Tricky and I used to joke about shopping at "dress for less" places. How the "name brands" are always "brands you've never heard of." Now I was surrounded by famous brands, and it was giving me a headache.

"Come on, Mieka," my aunt called. She was standing at the entrance to the dressing room, where the sales-lady had a roomful of stuff waiting for me. Dresses and shorts were draped over my aunt's arms, making her look like a haystack of clothes.

"Mieka!" Greta said as she hurried up to me. "Look at this skirt! You have to try it, it's so cute!"

"It's great," I agreed, angling my face to look at the skirt as we walked toward the dressing room. The one she was holding up was two sizes too small, but I didn't say anything.

"Oh, I'm so glad we're doing this." Aunt Kate nodded in approval at the skirt in Greta's hands as we stepped into the dressing room corridor. "Mieka honey, I know you're not exactly getting tons of fashion advice from your dad! Now, what do you want to start with? The yellow dress, maybe?"

But I didn't reply because my brain had momentarily shut down. I'd just had a thought, and it wouldn't make room for anything else. Here is the thought: they did this on purpose.

And the minute I thought it, I was sure that it was true. Aunt Kate didn't have anything to pick up at the mall. She just wanted to get me some clothes. She was trying to fix me.

I felt a little hurt, and for a minute I felt like I was betraying Dad. At the end of the dressing room was a long mirror. There I was—the "Before" picture in my jeans and ancient Mr. Bubble T-shirt, standing between two rows of white rooms, one of which was set up with a ton of new clothes.

And that was when I realized something: maybe I needed a little fixing. Grandma thought so. Arielle definitely thought so. And even Tricky had started to believe it. Besides, Aunt Kate had a point—my dad isn't exactly Captain Fashion. So where was the problem? Right?

"Yeah, I think I'll start with the dress," I said as I headed into one of the white doors on the left.

"Have a good time?" Uncle Dave asked as we walked

into the kitchen, laden with shopping bags. "Whoa. Looks like you bought out the store."

My dad placed the orange sports drink he had been chugging on the counter and looked at the bags, then at me. He and my uncle were both soaked with sweat— my dad's gray hair had turned dark with damp. His battered gray T-shirt had a small hole at the neck, and his red Converse high-tops were faded and dingy-looking. Dad's eyes didn't leave my face. "What's all this?"

I felt my face burn under his gaze.

"We bought a few things," Aunt Kate said breezily. "Mieka needed some clothes for the Houston heat."

"You should do a fashion show later," Greta suggested, elbowing me in the ribs.

My dad's eyes went round. "All of these things are for *Mieka*?" he asked. "*Just* Mieka?"

"Not all of them," Aunt Kate corrected.

Greta held up a black shopping bag the size of a deck of cards. "Mom got some eye shadow."

"Girls." Uncle Dave chuckled and rolled his eyes at my dad. "They've just got to go shopping, am I right?"

Dad looked like he was about to pass out. Suddenly, it was like a bandanna had been pulled from my eyes, and I saw the five huge shopping bags full of clothes the way Dad must be seeing them. What just happened? I thought.

"Mieka," he said slowly, "you'll have to return those clothes."

My heart spluttered and stopped, then started up again. I thought about the denim shorts in the bag—the tiny red flowers stitched on the pocket. "But Aunt Kate said—"

"Mieka." Dad's jaw went rigid—he was getting angry.

I looked to my aunt for help. "Jeff, she needs some new shorts, some light tops. It's hot here."

"Please, Dad," I begged. My yellow dress. I was so eager to wear it that I had to stop myself from running up to Greta's room to put it on right away. Who cares if we're not going anywhere? I thought.

My father swallowed hard. "How much do I owe you?" he asked Aunt Kate.

"Nothing!" she said cheerfully as she walked over to the fridge and pulled out a diet cola. "This is a gift for Mieka. We're just so happy to have her here for a visit." She smiled at me warmly and popped the top on the cola with a crack.

"I'll write you a check." My dad sounded as though his brain had been replaced with a computer chip.

"Give it up, Jeff-O," Uncle Dave said, pounding my father on the back. "We'll take care of this one."

"Mieka never would have needed these clothes if she hadn't come to Houston," my aunt argued. "Let us get them for her."

Dad shifted his weight from one foot to another and bit the skin at the edge of his thumb. He could see the names on the bags. He must have had some idea how much the clothes cost. My father managed to make a living as an artist—barely. We both knew that there was no way he could afford what was in the bags. No. Way. So here was his choice: make me return the stuff, or let me keep it. But what would be the point of making me take it back? I wondered. It would just hurt Aunt Kate's feelings . . . and mine.

Pleasepleasepleasepleaseplease, I begged silently. Please, Dad.

"Okay," my father said at last.

My breath swooshed out of me. Greta grinned.

"Mieka, thank your aunt and your uncle," he said.

"She thanked me about a thousand times already,"

Aunt Kate insisted, but it was too late. I'd already thrown my arms around her waist and said, "Thank you!" The bags in my hands crashed into each other briefly before I pulled away to rush over to my uncle. "Thank you, too!" I said as I hugged him. It was kind of a gross hug, given that he had just come from the gym, and everything, but I didn't care.

"You're welcome, hon." Uncle Dave patted my hair. "It's our pleasure."

chapter five

"Nana?"

"Sugarpop!" Something clattered at the other end of the line. "Oh, crud."

"The table?" I asked. I sat back against the pile of purple pillows on my bed. Everyone else was out in the pool, but I had asked Aunt Kate if I could call Nana.

"What else? Why don't I just clear this thing off, I ask you?" I heard Nana shuffling around, and I knew that she was putting the stack of papers and magazines back into place on top of the tiny telephone table in the corner of her kitchen. It was perched in such a way that if you jiggled it even slightly as you walked past, everything fell off and spilled onto the floor.

"Because you can't bear to part with your magazines." Nana loves magazines—especially housekeeping magazines. Her place was packed—cluttered—with articles on how to clear clutter and keep things neat. It's not that Nana is into housekeeping. She just thinks the magazines are beautiful, and can't bear to part with them.

"Never mind all of that—how's Houston?"

"Hot." I looked down at my new shorts. I had pulled them on over my swimsuit, which was kind of silly, considering that I was just going to take three steps outside and take them off in order to dive into the water. But I seriously could not wait one more minute to wear them.

"I was there once, and that's what I remember about it. Are you having fun with your cousins?"

"Sure." I didn't really want to talk about this. It wasn't like I was *not* having fun, exactly. How could I explain that I was just *all wrong* here? "How's everything there?"

"Oh, the usual." There was a loud squawk, and Nana said, "Oh, Uncle Walter, be quiet." I pictured her standing in the kitchen, wearing her usual summer outfit—a breezy dress and maroon Birkenstock sandals. It was a

Wednesday, so she would probably have her hair down. The store is closed on Wednesdays; it's Nana's day off.

"How's Uncle Walter?" I asked.

"Uncle Walter! Uncle Walter!" screeched a voice.

"He's being very naughty right now. Come down off the refrigerator, Uncle Walter," Nana begged. "Good boy," she added, and I knew that her parrot had fluttered onto her outstretched hand. She was probably carrying him over to the enormous white cage in the corner. Usually, Uncle Walter hangs out in the store with Nana while she's working. He has his own cage there, too, but he'll often perch on Nana's head, restlessly grooming her hair with his beak as she rings up customers. It always makes people laugh. Nana says that Uncle Walter is the best salesperson she's ever had. "Have you . . . seen your grandmother?"

There was just a slight hesitation in her voice, like maybe she wasn't sure she wanted to ask that question.

"Yep."

Pause.

"And?"

"She told me I was fat."

Nana groaned. "Oh Mieka, don't listen to her."

"Don't worry," I said.

"Your father's told me stories, sweetie. She can be really awful."

"I noticed."

Another pause.

"Is your dad okay?" Nana asked. It was funny to think about Grandma Baker—how she didn't seem like my dad's mother at all, while Nana did. I think that they really bonded when my mom moved to California.

It's funny how that works. I mean, I still get postcards from my mother every once in a while, and even the occasional e-mail. But I haven't seen her in two years. And I guess my dad is in the same situation with Grandma Baker.

"Grandma was mean to him, too, but he kind of seems used to it."

Nana cleared her throat. "That's a good way of putting it."

Pause, pause, pause.

It's weird how talking to Nana on the phone just isn't the same as talking to her in person. You'd think it would be kind of the same, but it isn't. "I wish I was there with you," I told her suddenly.

"Oh, sugarpop, me too." Nana's voice was so warm that tears threatened to strangle me.

I was filled with a sudden urge to be in my familiar old room, in our tiny little apartment filled with all of the stuff I knew by heart. Dad's blue bottle collection, my teddy bear—Herman—our oval coffee table with a coaster stuck under one leg, the black leather chair that feels like you're sinking into a warm hand . . . all of that stuff seemed very far away, like I'd only imagined it, or dreamed it, maybe.

I wished I were visiting Nana, instead of Grandma Baker. I tried to imagine Nana's face, but couldn't quite do it. I got a flash of dark eyes, long, shiny, silver hair, a nose as soft and pink as Silly Putty—but it didn't add up to Nana.

Through the window, I could see Aunt Kate reading by the pool as Greta and Mark splashed around.

Greta squinted up at me, shading her eyes with her hand. She waved, then beckoned for me to come down.

I nodded. "Hey, looks like I've got to go," I said to my grandmother.

"All right, sugarpop," Nana said. "I love you."

"I love you, too," I told her. I clicked off the phone

and sat there for a moment. Even though I was in Houston, with more family than I'd ever had before, I felt completely alone.

"Watch it, clumsy," Grandma Baker said to my dad as he tried to help Uncle Dave wheel her up the front steps.

"Don't worry, Mama Baker," Uncle Dave said. "We've got you."

"It's not *you* I'm worried about," Grandma snapped, glaring at her son.

Dad put his hands in the air and backed off to let Dave do the work of hauling Grandma. Sweat streaming down his face, my uncle grunted with the effort of dragging her wheelchair backward up the three front steps. I don't know how much she weighs, but she looked like one of those sea lions they have at the zoo, flopped into her wheelchair—you know, *dense*.

Of course, Dad is in way better shape than Uncle Dave, but Grandma didn't want anyone but my uncle to push her wheelchair around. When Greta tried to help out at the hospital, Grandma lit up like an ambulance— wailing and screeching.

Finally, Uncle Dave managed to get Grandma to the top landing and turn her around. "What in gravy is this?" she asked when she saw the WELCOME HOME banner hanging over the fireplace.

"We just wanted to let you know how glad we are that you're here," Aunt Kate said with a smile that looked like someone was punching her in the gut.

"Well, this isn't my home," Grandma grumbled.

Behind her, my dad shook his head.

"It is for now," Aunt Kate said.

Greta and I exchanged looks. I know she was thinking the same thing I was—how long is Grandma going to have to stay here? Poor Greta. I mean, at least I was leaving in two weeks.

"What's that look all about?" My grandmother was glaring at me.

"What?" I honestly didn't know what she was talking about. I mean, I had glanced over at Greta—but that was all. It wasn't even like I'd rolled my eyes, or anything.

"That *look*," Grandma sneered. Then she tucked in her chin and grimaced, lifting her eyeballs to the ceiling. I guess she was imitating my expression, but she looked like a gargoyle with a serious case of indigestion. "Wipe that look off your face. You, too," she snapped at Greta.

"Sorry," Greta said meekly.

"Sorry," Grandma mimicked in a whiney mosquito voice. "I'm tired," she announced after a moment. "Take me to my room, David."

"Will do—urgh." That last part was the grunt my uncle gave as he started pushing Grandma in the direction of the guest room. The rest of us trailed behind. Mark looked longingly at the front door, as if he was thinking about running through it and never coming back.

Grandma scanned the room appraisingly as she reached into her bag. "Well, I guess some people like yellow," she said as she pulled a pack of cigarettes out of her purse and shook one into her hand.

Aunt Kate's eyebrows shot up in shock. "Mother, you can't smoke anymore."

"Who says?" Grandma asked as she clicked a lighter, touching the flame to the end of her cigarette.

"The doctor!"

"That doctor doesn't even speak English," Grandma

shot back as a double stream of blue smoke poured from her nostrils.

I was wondering if she was talking about the same doctor who had been there earlier when we picked Grandma up from the hospital. He was Indian—or maybe Pakistani—and he had an accent. But he spoke perfect English, as far as I could tell.

Aunt Kate folded her arms across her chest, glowering. "Dr. Banghadar is one of the most experienced cardiac—"

"Oh, Kate, come on," Uncle Dave said softly. "Here Mama Baker, let me open a window." The room had already filled up with the stink of cigarette smoke. I wished burning cigarettes smelled nice, the way burning wood does. Nana's friend, Grace, is a smoker, and her clothes always smell stale and old. She tries to cover it up with perfume, but that just makes everything worse.

"Thank you, David," Grandma said. "May I have an ashtray?"

"No, because we don't have any ashtrays," Aunt Kate said. "And if you smoke, you could have a relapse—"

Grandma lifted her eyebrows at her daughter. "Then I'll take a glass with about a half an inch of water in it."

"That is disgusting," Aunt Kate said as she walked out of the room.

"Smoking is bad for you," Mark piped up.

"I'm not going to worry about that while I'm on my deathbed," Grandma said.

With a snort, my dad retreated down the hall. He'd been disappearing into his room a lot lately. To work on his painting, he said. I knew he had a new book cover due soon. Some dragon thing. I couldn't wait to get a look at the canvas. My dad paints amazing dragons.

A moment later, Aunt Kate reappeared holding a glass. A small amount of water swirled around the bottom. "I can't believe I'm doing this," she said as she placed the glass on Grandma's bedside table. Grandma flicked her cigarette against the edge, and gray ash fell into the water, like poison fish flakes.

"All right, Mama Baker," Uncle Dave said. "We'll let you rest a little."

Grandma looked at him gratefully. "Honestly, David, I don't know what this family would do without you," she said. Weirdly, she actually sounded like she meant it. She didn't say anything to Aunt Kate.

"Come on, kids," Aunt Kate said, turning to go. "Let's go for a swim."

"Can I have a Popsicle?" Mark asked.

"You can have dessert after dinner," my aunt told him, putting her hands behind his shoulders to nudge him out of the room. "You can have a granola bar or a piece of fruit instead."

"But why can't I—"

"Did you hear what I said?" Aunt Kate snapped, her eyes flashing angrily. "I said *no*. I'm *sick* of arguing." She nearly spat the word "sick," like it really made her want to cough something up. But the weird thing was, I hadn't seen her argue with Mark once in the past week.

Mark bit his lip. His chin quivered a little, but he didn't cry.

"Come on, chief," Uncle Dave said, patting him on the arm. "I'll race you to the pool."

Nodding, Mark shuffled out of the room. He didn't look like he wanted to race, though.

Grandma Baker looked out the window, inhaling her

cigarette deeply. The blinds cast bars across her face, like she was in prison, or a cage at the zoo. Smoke poured from her nose, dragon-like. I imagined her spewing flames on all of us, turning us to cinders.

Uncle Dave closed the door with a quiet snick. Aunt Kate massaged the ridge above her right eye, like she had a horrible headache. We should hang a sign on the doorknob, I thought. BEWARE OF GRANDMA.

chapter six

The squealing started the minute we stepped out of the car.

"Omigosh, Gretaaaaaaaaaa!" A plump blond girl bounded over to us and wrapped my cousin into a huge bear hug.

"Gretaaaaa!" A girl with streaky gold highlights in her dark hair and suspiciously pink cheeks wrapped her arms around both of them.

"Omigosh, hi-i-i-i-i, y'all!" Greta started squealing along, and all three girls started jumping up and down. Wow. Greta had missed only a week of camp, and her friends were going bananas.

"My ears," Mark complained from the backseat. He

was going to some camp for geniuses, and was getting dropped off later. Lucky kid. Reaching out, he yanked the door closed with a slam. I saw Aunt Kate wave just before she pulled away. Take me with you! I wanted to shout, but I didn't dare. After all, did I really want to spend the day with Grandma, watching her blow streams of smoke from her nose like a bitter dragon? No, thanks. So I had to come to day camp with Greta. No big.

"Kristin Taylor and Julie Chin, this is my cousin, Mieka Baker." The smiley girls smiled harder. So these were Greta's friends—the ones she'd been chatting with online. They looked just like Greta—with perfectly brushed hair and tidy little outfits, as if they had just stepped out of the manufacturer's plastic box they had been living in for the past twelve years.

"I'm from Boston," I said. I have no idea why. It came out sounding really dumb, and instantly I wished that I could TiVo my life, hit the rewind button, say something—anything—else.

"Oh, Boston," Kristin—the blond one—said. "My dad went to Harvard." She said it like maybe he'd given her a teddy bear in a Harvard T-shirt when she was born, or something. I knew some people did that—they thought their children's lives would be over if their kids didn't follow in their Harvardy footsteps. She sounded as though the idea of Boston made her kind of ill.

Julie didn't respond to my comment at all. "Greta, Ellie wants us over by the snack shack," she said. Julie grabbed Greta's hand, and Greta grabbed mine and Kristin grabbed Julie's, and off we went.

Okay, I have to admit it—as we walked along, I couldn't help noticing that I was hanging out with the Pretties. I wondered what Arielle and Tricky would say if they could see this. I felt kind of cool and kind of self-conscious at the same time, like I'd been miscast.

We snaked down a dirt path toward a small building made of logs. The nice thing about this day camp was that it wasn't so god-awful hot. I mean, it was hot—don't get me wrong. But there were lots of big shady trees, and we were catching a nice breeze, so it didn't feel as bad.

"Hey, Tenners!" A tall, slim woman with short black hair smiled at me. She looked superathletic, like maybe she'd just left the U.S. women's soccer team to work at this camp, or something. "Who's this?"

"Ellie, this is my cousin Mieka," Greta piped up. "She's staying with us for a while."

"Mieka Baker, that's right. We were expecting you. Grrrreat!" Ellie said "great" with a little trill on the r, like she really, really meant it. "Welcome to Group Ten. This is Roxie, Meg, and Tanner," she said, pointing to three other kids. Roxie had curly black hair and masses of freckles all over her body. Meg had a round face and strawberry blond hair. Tanner had big hazel eyes and a really bad haircut, and could have been a boy or a girl. It was hard to tell.

"Where's Kelli?" Meg asked.

"She's on Kelli time." Roxie shrugged. "She'll get here twenty minutes late, as usual."

"Here comes Group Nine," Ellie said, waving. "Hey, Charlie!"

A hunky surfer-looking guy with floppy hair waved back and shouted, "Ellie!" as he trotted over to us, trailed by seven guys. Well, I realized later that there must have been seven, because at that moment, I was struck with temporary blindness. I could see only one of them.

He had curly brown hair and huge brown eyes

rimmed with long lashes, longer than a girl's, and was wearing a faded blue polo shirt and khaki shorts. I felt like something heavy had just landed on my head. Serious, instantaneous crush.

And then the most incredible thing happened. He took one look at me and said, "Hey—were you here last week?"

"Yeah, who's the new girl?" A dark-skinned boy grinned at me, flashing white teeth.

"I'm Mieka," I said, absently tracing my fingers over the embroidered flowers on my shorts.

"She's from Boston," Kristin said, and Julie punched her in the arm, which made the two of them crack up.

I felt the blood rise to my face. So I really *had* sounded like an idiot.

"Boston? Are you lost?" The dark-skinned boy's black eyes twinkled above his slim, pointed nose.

"Be quiet, Shaz," Crush Boy said.

"She's my cousin," Greta piped up.

"Yeah? Cool." My crush had a short scar that cut through the center of his left eyebrow. I wondered how he got it, and what it would be like to trace my finger-tip over it.

"Okay, Peter, enough with the question-and-answer session." Charlie yanked out a clipboard. "After chapel, we've got a team challenge. Orange doughnut in groups of seven."

A general cheer rose from the group while I was still thinking—*chapel*? Then Greta nudged me, mouthing the word *doughnut*. So, I was about to see the mysterious orange doughnut. I couldn't wait to tell Dad.

"Look who's finally here." Ellie was peering down the dirt road, where a tall girl was running toward us. She had superlong legs, and her skin was deep brown. I couldn't help noticing the muscles in her calves. Everyone here was so fit—it was starting to make me nervous.

"Kelli!" Shaz shouted as she ran over.

"Sorrysorrysorry!" Kelli called as she joined the group. She and Shaz pounded fists. "What did I miss?"

"Almost chapel," Ellie said. Then she lifted her hand over her head, pointed forward, and started walking down a road paved with dry dust.

Both groups trooped after Ellie. As we walked, Julie started singing a song about a crazy billboard that got all messed up in a thunderstorm. Everyone joined in—

except for me. I didn't know the words, and even though I tried to catch some of them, they whizzed past like windblown snowflakes.

Eventually, we came to a small hill. A flat space was carved out at the foot of the hill, and a young guy with sandy hair and blue eyes was standing there, greeting people as they streamed past.

He whooped when he saw us. "Group Ten!" he shouted. Then, pointing to Charlie, he added, "And Group Nine!"

Everyone in my group let out a shout, taking me by surprise. Oh, we're cheering again, I realized. "Whoo!" I shouted, a beat too late. Everyone cracked up.

Greta punched me in the arm playfully and Kristin rolled her eyes as we climbed into the bleachers, which were really railroad ties set into the side of the hill.

"That's Pastor Mike," Greta whispered as the young guy shouted out to Group One—the littlest kids. He gave a small boy, whose face was almost completely hidden by his cotton-ball hair, a high five, laughing, as the kids cheered.

"It's the start of another great week at Camp Franklin!" Pastor Mike shouted, punching his fist in the air. "And how do we feel about it?"

The bleachers erupted. It reminded me of Fenway Park, where the Red Sox play. It was amazing how much noise a group of about seventy kids could make. Kristin and Julie were stomping their feet. Greta put her fingers in her mouth and let out a loud whistle.

Wow. I'd always wanted to be able to do that.

Eventually, everyone quieted down, and Pastor Mike led us in a song. It was a round, and the words were—lucky for me—completely simple. We just sang, "Love is here, love is there, love is every, everywhere," over and over, and it was really pretty. Then Pastor Mike asked for four volunteers to act out a story from the New Testament.

I tried to make myself invisible, but he pointed to me right away. "I don't think I've seen you before."

"She's new!" Ellie shouted helpfully. "An out-of-town visitor for the next two weeks!"

"A visitor!" Pastor Mike's eyebrows zipped to the top of his forehead, practically. "Hey, everyone, how do we feel about visitors?"

The crowd—naturally—let out a crazy cheer. In my heart, I felt like if Pastor Mike had shouted, "Hey, everyone, how do we feel about salamanders?" the campers would have gone equally nuts. Still, the cheer gave me a warm feeling, vibrating in my chest. Two rows in front of me, Peter had turned in his seat to give me a huge grin.

"What's your name, special guest star?" Pastor Mike called.

"I'm Mieka," I told him.

"Okay, Mieka, come on down here." He crooked his finger at me, giving me a huge wink.

I hesitated, and Greta elbowed me in the ribs. "Go on down there," she said.

I swallowed hard, feeling hopelessly shy. "I—"

"What's wrong?" Kristin asked, leaning across Julie to talk to Greta.

"Don't you want to?" Julie asked. She blinked her dark eyes blankly, as if she couldn't believe that I might not want to act out a Bible story in front of a bunch of people.

My brain was screaming: I don't know any Bible stories! But I didn't want to say so.

"Of course she does," Greta said, touching my arm. "You're so lucky! I *never* get picked."

I didn't want Greta's friends to think I was weird, so I stood up. The crowd cheered as I walked down the center aisle and stood next to Pastor Mike. I swear I heard Greta shout, "Go, Mieka!" and let out a loud, long whistle.

Pastor Mike picked out three more volunteers. Peter was one, and I felt my ears throb with my heartbeat when he came and stood next to me. Okay, so whatever we're doing can't be *that* bad, I thought. At least it involves standing close to the crushiest guy in the universe.

Next up was a girl in Group Four named April, and then one of the Group Oners—a seven-year-old named Stanley. Stanley was missing two front teeth, and was really excited to be chosen, which was why he was a little disappointed to learn that all he was supposed to do was lie on the ground.

"It's a very important part," Pastor Mike told him. "You have to lie very still, okay, Stanley?"

Stanley sighed dramatically. "All right," he said, flopping onto the dirt.

"Okay, everybody else, just follow along and do what I say." Pastor Mike gestured for us to stand to the side and wait for his signal. "Peter, you're the priest. And April, you're the religious woman. And Mieka—you'll be our Samaritan."

I had no idea what a Samaritan was, but I decided to play along. Just pretend you're Greta, I thought. "Gotcha," I said.

Mike rubbed his hands together and raised his voice. "Okay, everyone! So—once upon a time, a man was robbed and left for dead in the middle of the road." Pastor Mike gestured toward Stanley, who waved to the crowd. Everyone cracked up.

Pastor Mike cleared his throat. "He was very seriously injured," he said, nudging Stanley gently with a sandaled toe.

Stanley closed his eyes and lay still.

"So—along came a priest!" Pastor Mike gestured toward Peter, who walked toward Stanley. "But the priest didn't help the man!"

The crowd booed as Peter stuck his nose in the air and walked away, which made me giggle.

"Next came a religious woman," Pastor Mike said, gesturing toward April. "But she ignored the poor injured man, as well."

April skipped past Stanley, and everyone laughed and booed at her.

"Then along came a Samaritan!" Pastor Mike said, smiling at me with his twinkly eyes.

I stepped forward.

"Now, what you have to understand is that everyone thought that Samaritans were bad people," Pastor Mike said. Bad people—got it, I thought as I started to walk past Stanley, but Pastor Mike grabbed my sleeve. "But this was a good Samaritan! She looked at the man and saw that he was still alive!"

What? Oh! I bent over Stanley and pretended to feel his pulse. I put my hands to my face to indicate that I was shocked that he wasn't dead.

"So she picked him up and carried him down the road," Pastor Mike said.

I stared at Pastor Mike, and he nodded encouragingly. I looked down at Stanley, who was squinting up at me, still pretending to be dead. He wasn't that big. . . .

Shrugging, I bent down and scooped up Stanley. The crowd cheered wildly as I staggered off with him. It wasn't easy to hold him, since Stanley was giggling like mad.

"Oh, man, you're cool!" Peter laughed as I set Stanley down.

Stanley dusted off his shirt. "That was fun!" he said as Peter offered me a high five.

His palm was warm as I slapped it.

"Okay, everyone, let's give a round of applause to our volunteers!" Pastor Mike said.

I couldn't stop grinning as I made my way to my seat. The Pretties were cheering madly, and Greta hugged me as I sat down next to her. "That was great!" she said, laughing. "I can't believe you picked him up!"

"He wasn't that heavy," I told her. My face almost ached with my smile.

I had just acted out a Bible story, and it was actually . . . fun. I wondered what my dad would think of that.

"Okay, everyone. Group challenge time!" Ellie announced once chapel was over. "We're heading down to the tire swing." We were standing in a little cluster with Group Nine at the top of the hill. "Everyone count off in twos. Ones with me, twos with Charlie."

I'm not sure how they did it, but the Pretties spread out so that once we had counted off, I found myself in a group with Greta, Julie, Kristin, Kelli, Shaz, this mop-headed guy named Mark, and Peter.

"Here we are," Ellie chirped as we reached the trunk of a ginormous tree. I was about to ask where the doughnut was, when I happened to glance up. The "doughnut" was a round orange piece of rubber tied to a high branch, suspended about ten feet off the ground. It looked like a tire swing, but smaller.

"How do you swing on it?" I asked, which was—apparently—a pretty good joke, because it made everyone crack up.

"This is a team challenge," Ellie explained. "You have to work together to get everyone through the doughnut safely, one at a time."

Through it? I did not like the sound of this. Not at all. It must have showed on my face, because Greta leaned over and whispered, "We did it last year. It's really not as hard as it sounds."

I nodded at Greta, which was bad timing on my part, because it so happened that Ellie had just asked, "Would anyone like to go first?" So when she saw my head bobbing up and down, she said, "Okay, Mieka! Grrrreat!"

Save me, I thought desperately, but Peter was smiling his supercute smile at me and Greta gave me a little shove forward and suddenly I found myself at the center of the group. I could feel seven sets of eyes boring into my skull. I looked up at the tire. It seemed a million miles away, like maybe it was swinging from another planet. "Okay," I said finally. "Uh, what do I do?"

"Pete, lace your fingers together," Shaz said. "Like this. Mieka, step into my hands, then step into Peter's. We'll lift you toward the swing."

"Oh, no," I said. There were so many reasons that was a bad idea. What if I had something gross on the bottom of my shoe and it got on Peter's hand? Would he be able to feel how much I weigh? Oh, jeez, this was just too humiliating.

"Seriously, this is the only way." Shaz gestured at me with his interlaced hands. "Step up."

I cast a "Help me" glance at Greta, but she just clapped her hands and shouted, "Go, Mieka!"

Julie took up the cheer. "You can do it!" She let out a whoop, and in the next moment, everyone was cheering for me

I wanted to find a hole to crawl into and simply wait for death.

But there were no good-size holes nearby, so I stuck my foot in Shaz's hands, then balanced my palm against his skull while I stepped into Peter's hands. Grunting, they started to lift me toward the swing, but I was shaky. Tilting wildly to the right, I windmilled my arms and tried to regain my balance.

"Ouch!" Shaz cried as I grabbed his hair.

"Sorry!"

Peter grunted as he lifted his hands toward his chest, and in the next moment, my fingers brushed the tire swing. Suddenly, I had a grip on it, and as the two boys lifted me higher, I got one arm through the tire, then the other. A whoop went up from my team as I pulled myself halfway through.

I'm doing it! I thought. I'm actually doing this impossible thing!

I reached my hands down and Kelli grabbed one while Peter grabbed the other. They yanked, and the swing tilted a little, bringing my face perpendicular to the ground.

I let out a little grunt and shimmied forward an inch,

but something was wrong. Here was the bad news—
I couldn't move. My butt was stuck in the orange
doughnut.

"Just pull yourself through!" Greta shouted up at me.
"You can do it, Mieka!"

I wanted to kill her. Here I was, holding the hand of
the boy of my dreams, with my heinie permanently
pressed into a swing. What is it with all of these bean-
poles? I wondered. Am I really the only girl with hips at
this camp? I gawked down at Greta, Kristin, Julie, and
Kelli. Hmm, I thought. Maybe so.

I tried to go backward. No go. I was hanging
through that orange rubber tire like a damp sock, and
the angle was so awkward that I couldn't move at all.
I felt the blood rushing to my head.

Did you know that you can actually die of embar-
rassment? I know this for a fact, because I felt myself
dying at that very moment. Passing into the next
life. . . .

"We've got you!" Kelli cried. "We'll all catch you!"

Just tell them that you're stuck, my reasonable mind
said. But I couldn't. Not with Peter standing right there.
Not with my perfect cousin leading the cheering section.

"She's not even trying," Kristin mumbled.

I glared at her.

"I'm spotting the group," Ellie reassured me. "Don't be afraid."

That's it! Ellie had just fed me the perfect line. "I—I'm afraid of heights," I lied. "I don't think I can do this."

"Yes you can!" Greta cheered. "Come on, Mieka! No fear!"

A moment later, everyone else was cheering and whooping. "You need to overcome your fears, Mieka," Ellie called. "That's what the team challenge is all about!"

Great. This was even worse than before.

"Really, I can't," I said in my most reasonable voice.

They went on whooping and cheering for a while, but I just hung there over their heads like the star of a budget version of *Peter Pan* until Kelli and then Peter let go of my hands. Eventually, Ellie had to give up. She called Charlie over, and everyone in both groups got to watch as the counselors untied the rope and slowly lowered me to the ground.

Once I wasn't hanging, I managed to wriggle out of

the tire. My stomach was sore. Frowning, Ellie looked at her watch. "Looks like our team flunks the challenge for today."

The team groaned.

"I'm sorry," I told her. I snuck a glance a Peter, who was shaking his head.

"It means we have to clear the dishes for other groups at lunch," Kelli explained.

"It's not her fault," Greta said loyally. "Everyone's afraid of something." She patted me on the back. "Don't worry about it," she said. "There'll be another team challenge tomorrow."

Great. That was exactly what I was afraid of.

chapter seven

When Aunt Kate picked us up later that day, Mark was slouched in the way-backseat, glowering out the window. Grandma was in the front passenger seat. She didn't even crack a smile when she saw us.

"Hi, girls!" Aunt Kate chirped. "Did you have a great time?"

"A blast," Greta said as we climbed into the SUV.

"That's what I like to hear!" Aunt Kate adjusted the rearview mirror so that she could grin at us. "How about you, Mieka?"

"It was good," I said. Well, parts of it were good. Everything but the orange doughnut was good.

"Just good?" Aunt Kate's face darkened—it was

pretty clear that I'd said the wrong thing. Anything less than total enthusiasm seemed to get on my aunt's nerves.

I corrected myself. "It was great."

"Actually, Mom, Mieka had a really scary experience on the doughnut challenge. She's afraid of heights."

"What?" Aunt Kate glanced at me in the rearview mirror.

Remind me to strangle you later, I thought at Greta. "It wasn't a big deal. I was supposed to go through the tire and come down head first, but I was too scared to try it."

Grandma snorted from the front seat. "More like you were too afraid to go on a diet."

"Mother!"

"Don't mind me," Grandma said as she looked out the window. "Nobody does."

I could feel my cousin's eyes on my face. I wished I could do something to stop the blush that was spreading across my cheeks, but I knew it was hopeless. My secret was out. Thanks, Grandma.

I guess my aunt felt a little sorry for me, because she picked up a postcard that was lying on the dashboard and handed it to me. "Mieka, you got some real mail."

"Ooh, lucky!" Greta peeked at the picture, which was of one of the swan boats that float on the river that runs through Boston Common.

Dear Sugarpop,
Missing you! I've taught Uncle Walter how to say, "Where's Mieka?" Now he won't stop.
Love,
Nana

"Who's it from?" Greta asked.

"Nana," I said, tucking the postcard into my back pocket. I cast a quick glance at Mark, who was watching me carefully from the backseat. His eyes flicked out the window when I caught him looking at me. "She misses me."

"So she says," Grandma muttered.

"Of course she misses you," Aunt Kate said, and I wondered if she had read the postcard.

I wished that it was Nana in the front seat instead of Grandma. If I told her about the orange doughnut, she would have understood.

Greta and Aunt Kate spent the ride home chatting about camp. Greta gave the real play-by-play—she related the name of every single song and talked about every single activity. I was pretty impressed that she could remember so many details—and even more impressed that Aunt Kate actually seemed interested in hearing them. "So, Mom, do you think you could come for Parents' Day? It's Friday after next."

"I'll have to check, sweetie," Kate said, steering into the driveway.

"What do you have to check?" Grandma Baker demanded. "It's not like you have a job."

Aunt Kate's jaw tightened, but she didn't say anything to her mother. She just pulled up in front of the house and parked the car suddenly, so that it gave a slight jerk when it came to a stop.

I looked up at the wide wooden door. It was enormous and beautiful, just like the rest of the house. Even after living there for over a week, I was still surprised by the size of the place every time we pulled up in front of it. It was a huge brick building, three stories tall. My cousins lived in a leafy neighborhood called River Oaks. It was a really pretty place. The houses had huge landscaped yards bursting with flowers in shocking pink, electric blue, vibrant purple, and greens so green it made your mouth water. Each one of these houses was bigger than the white stone apartment buildings in Nana's neighborhood.

"Is my dad around?" I asked as we walked into the cool entryway and past the living room that nobody used. The super air-conditioning felt wonderful after spending the whole day outside.

"In his room, I think," Aunt Kate said as Grandma wheezed into the front hall after her. "He's been painting all day."

"Want to go for a swim?" Greta asked me. She didn't bother asking Mark—he was skulking up the stairs to his room.

"What's with him?" I asked her.

She just shrugged. "So, do you want to go?"

"Just let me say hi to my dad and I'll meet you." I couldn't wait to sneak a peek at my dad's dragon.

"Yeah?" Dad asked as I knocked softly at the door. Weird. He sounded annoyed. Usually, when he's working, his voice goes soft and dreamy. Maybe I'm interrupting him, I thought.

"It's me," I said softly.

"Oh, Mieka!" Dad opened the door and smiled an apology. "Come in, come in." He had a paintbrush in his hand, and another one stuck behind his ear.

"I can come back later," I told him.

"No, no." Dad laughed, but it wasn't a happy laugh. "You're not interrupting anything."

I looked around the room, where Dad had set up a tidy little table with brushes and paint. His easel was propped up near the window, with the canvas facing the natural light. It was pretty far from his usual chaos. At home, Dad's studio is a beautiful mess of gorgeous drawings taped to the walls, shelves and shelves of paint, paintings stacked ten deep on the floor, half-formed collages, manuscripts, models of all sorts of magical creatures for reference, and photographs. It definitely seemed like my dad was working with the "travel pack," like those tiny toothpastes and shampoos you get for your toiletries bag.

"Can I take a look?" I asked, gesturing to the easel.

Dad hesitated, then barked a little laugh. "Knock yourself out," he said.

I stepped across the room, careful not to bump

anything on the table, and stood to face the painting. When I saw the canvas, I stood perfectly still for a moment, trying to take in what I was looking at.

"It's blank," I said.

"Well, technically, it's covered in a layer of white gesso," Dad corrected. He smiled with only half of his mouth.

I wasn't sure what I was supposed to say. He'd been working on the painting for a week. "Um . . . it's very evenly applied."

Dad laughed. "Yeah." He dropped the brush he was holding onto the table. "I'm sure Veronica will love it." Veronica was the art director my dad worked with most often.

"It's minimalist," I joked. "A minimalist dragon."

"That's what I'll tell her." Dad nodded as he sat on the bed. "It leaves more to the reader's imagination."

I sat down next to him, and the pull-out bed bounced slightly.

"I kept painting over what I had," Dad said finally. "I couldn't make it work. The whole thing looked stiff, unnatural." My father is always saying that the secret to illustrating fantasy is that you have to make things look even more real than they look in real life. "After a while, the canvas was lumpy and covered with blotches, so I decided to start again."

"Probably a good idea," I said.

Dad looked at the easel. "I guess." His face went sort of blank, and I felt his mind going over and over, the gears grinding, trying to find a solution to his problem. After a moment, he turned to me. "How was camp?"

"Kind of a disaster," I admitted.

"Really?" Dad asked. He seemed genuinely surprised to hear this.

I sighed.

"Do you . . . you don't have to go back, if you don't want," my dad said. "If it isn't fun."

I thought about my dad's lumpy canvas—how he couldn't get it to turn out right, so he was just going to start over. A fresh start. Maybe that was what I needed to do at camp. I could just try a little harder, be a little more enthusiastic. Like Greta. Besides, what was my option? Hang out with Grandma, bringing her ashtrays all day?

"I think I'll give it another try," I said at last. "The people were nice."

Dad wrapped his arm around my shoulder. "That's my girl," he said.

"You're reading *that*?" Grandma asked when Mark trotted up to me with a book in his hand. At dinner, he'd asked me to read him a story, and I hadn't felt like I could say no.

Mark climbed onto the couch and snuggled beside me, like he was my pet. "I like the pictures."

I looked down at the book. *Cinderella.*

"What's wrong with this story?" I asked.

I didn't mean to sound rude, I swear I didn't, because I am being on my Best Behavior, but she glared at me as though I was the most ridiculous person in the world.

Outside the window, a silver flash caught my eye. Greta was twirling her baton. She's on some kind of baton twirling team at school. The silver rod flashed as she sent it around her body in an endlessly spinning motion. I wondered what it would be like to be so coordinated.

"A boy should want to hear stories about trucks . . . or trains," Grandma told Mark. "Besides, at your age, you should be reading on your own."

Mark's face turned bright red. I hated her for it, but Grandma had a point. Aunt Kate always said that Mark was a genius. But I know that I could read by myself at Mark's age. Still, I wasn't about to let her *know* that she had a point.

"Sometimes people just like to be read to. Right, Mark?" I said.

His little round face looked up at me gratefully. "Right."

Case closed, I thought as I flipped open the book. "'Once upon a time, there was a beautiful little girl named Cinderella,'" I started.

Grandma snorted. I considered telling her to go get her own story, but instead I just read on.

"What do you think they talked about?" Mark asked when I came to the part about the prince.

"Who?"

"Cinderella and the prince," he said. "At the ball. How do you think he fell in love with her so fast?"

Wow—I'd never really thought about that. Had they even talked at all? The pictures just showed them gazing into each other's eyes. And at the end of the night, the prince didn't even know Cinderella's name. He didn't know anything about her, in fact—like that she lived in an attic and had close personal relationships with mice.

"He fell in love with her because she was gorgeous," Grandma sneered. "That's all."

"And because she was nice," Mark insisted. "The book said so. Didn't it, Mieka?"

"Yeah, that's what it said." And it had said that. But I'm not sure I believed it. Her inner beauty was just kind of a lucky coincidence for the prince. I mean, if Cinderella had been as ugly as the evil stepsisters, would he have fallen for her? Probably not. He would have fallen in love with some other pretty girl.

Mark sighed as he traced his fingers over the image of the prince and Cinderella, riding off into the sunset in their new non-pumpkin–shaped coach. "She's so pretty," Mark said, wrinkling his eyebrows.

Outside, the baton flashed like a silver wheel as Greta spun it around, around, and flipped it into the air, then caught it without even looking. Her face was pink with effort, her hair half out of her French braid as she practiced, but she still looked beautiful. Greta always looked beautiful. She could wear a burlap sack and a potato on her head, and she would still look beautiful. That's why she hung out with the other Pretties—that's just who they were. It was just so unfair.

Here is my question—am I the only person on earth who understands why the stepsisters hated Cinderella so much?

chapter eight

"Okay, everyone, here's what we're doing." The counselor with long brown curls smiled and held up a book. Her name was Jewel, and she sort of looked like a jewel. Her skin was a deep gold color and her eyes were hazel, and she had a kind of gentle, dreamy way of talking that made her heavy accent sound like music. "Today, we're working on illustration." Opening the book, she revealed the craziest picture I thought I'd ever seen. I guess it was supposed to be a picture of Hell—it had all of these little naked figures in a pool of flame looking up at a hideous yuck-faced ghoul. "Hieronymus Bosch," Jewel said, and I didn't know if she was giving us the name of the artist or was just saying something in a foreign language. She held up another illustration. This one was of two figures reaching toward each other. One was a handsome, muscular young man, and the other one was a handsome, muscular old man. They seemed to be floating in the sky, and there was just a tiny patch of blue between their outstretched index fingers. "Michelangelo." Jewel gave the picture a lingering, affectionate smile before closing the book and reaching for another. She held up a black-and-white drawing—an etching, it turned out. Four men on horses were trampling a crowd of desperate-looking people as an angel flew above them. They were carrying weapons—swords, arrows—and one carried scales. The old-fashioned kind you weigh things on—the kind that blindfolded Justice is always holding up in pictures. The picture was miserable and terrifying at the same time. "Albrecht Dürer," Jewel said.

"All of these artists got their inspiration from the same place—the Bible. So that's what I want you to do. Choose a favorite story or moment in the Bible, and really imagine it, then draw that scene. I have lots of magazines for visual reference, if you need it. Let me know if you need any help."

I ran my hand across the smooth white paper that lay on the table in front of me and thought of my dad's painting. My finger left a dirt smudge near the top right corner, and in that moment, I understood Dad's problem. The white paper was so perfect that anything I put on it would just mess it up. Besides, I didn't know any Bible stories. I wanted Jewel to come over so that I could explain that I didn't really go to church, but she was busy talking to Kristin, showing her a picture in a magazine.

Beside me, Greta was already carving away at her paper. She gripped her marker like she wanted to stab someone with it, with a tight fist. On the page, a gray blob with a snake coming out of the edge was slowly coming to life. "What are you drawing?" I asked.

"Noah's ark," she said to the paper as she drew another gray blob-snake combination. I realized suddenly that those shapes were supposed to be elephants, or at least their heads.

Noah's ark. Okay, that was one Bible story I'd heard of. But now Greta was doing that one, and I didn't want to rip off her idea.

Bible story, Bible story . . . Looking around, I saw all

of the other campers drawing away. Kelli had a pile of *National Geographic* magazines and was flipping through the pages so carefully that it looked like she was trying to find Waldo, or something. What is she looking for? I wondered. Why didn't my dad ever take me to church? I'd never really wondered before. This camp was making me feel like a religion reject.

When I thought of the Bible, I just thought of a dusty book that nobody really read. I thought of men in robes with long beards walking around in sandals healing people. Like the Good Samaritan. That was a cool story, but it didn't really make for a good picture for the arts shack, you know? It lacked a certain . . . pizzazz.

I toyed with the idea of asking Greta for help. Toyed with it the way a cat toys with a mouse—I kept letting it go and then catching hold of it again. Greta knows a lot of Bible stuff, I thought. But I felt kind of—well— dumb for not knowing any stories. Peter and Shaz were at the table next to ours, chatting in low voices. Shaz looked over at me, and I glued my eyes back to my paper. I didn't want Peter to know that I was sitting here without a clue.

"Stuck?" Smelling of roses and bug spray, Jewel slipped onto the bench beside me. That's when I noticed that she had a small gold nose ring and a tattoo running up her shoulder. It looked like letters, but I couldn't read them because her sleeve hid most of it. "Don't look at the whiteness—it makes your brain blank out."

"Tell me about it." I rubbed my crumbly block of white eraser against the smudge in the corner, and succeeded in adding a black smear to the paper.

"In Persia, the ancient artists always included a mistake in their rugs," Jewel said, eyeing the smudge/ streak. "They thought that making something perfect was a sign of pride."

"Well, I'm so talented that I can do that without even trying."

Jewel laughed so hard that Meg—who was sitting across the table from me—looked up from her drawing to see what the giggling was about.

"What's so funny?"

"Mieka," Jewel said, which made me feel like a bubble in a fizzy drink. I forced myself not to glance at Peter's table.

"Okay, look, if you're stuck, why don't you start by naming a few stories," Jewel suggested. "Then you can just pick one."

I winced. "I don't really know too many Bible stories."

"Don't you know *any*?" Jewel asked. Like she didn't believe me.

"Well . . ." I ransacked my brain, picking up thoughts and shoving them aside, making a huge mess.

"You don't know anything about the Bible?" Meg was shocked, like she'd just found out that I was from Planet Freakulon, or something.

Greta looked over at me, then at my blank page, then looked down at her own work. Embarrassed for me.

"Well, you know Noah's ark," Jewel prompted, gesturing to Greta's drawing, where a yellow blob on a pole (giraffe?) stood on a large brown half-circle (ark?). "And you know Delilah cut off Samson's hair, and you know Daniel in the lion's den."

"She doesn't know them," Meg said. "Look at her."

"Of course I do," I lied. I cleared my throat.

"No, you don't," Meg shot back. "Aren't you Christian?"

I wasn't really sure how to answer that. My dad was raised Episcopalian. Kind of. But he didn't go to church anymore. And my mother was Jewish. What did that make me—both? Jewpiscopalian? I wasn't sure. I didn't feel like either.

Jewel wasn't fazed. "Jonah and the whale?" she tried.

"Oh!" I said, because that was a story that shot a spark through my mind. I tried to follow it, but it blinked out, like a firefly.

I think Jewel read my mind. "Everyone on the ship thinks Jonah is a jinx, and then he gets swallowed by a whale. . . ."

"Right." The firefly blinked on again. I had it. I knew what I would draw. "Thanks," I said as I grabbed a stick of charcoal from the basket in front of me. *The Four Horsemen of the Apocalypse* swirled before my eyes, and I decided that my drawing would be in black and white. No colorful markers for Jonah. His is a pretty sad story, anyway.

Quickly, like Dad does, I outlined the prow of the boat, and a figure standing at the edge, looking into the distance. On the horizon, I drew a whale, its mouth open in a yawn so that seawater is spilling in, curling into the corners in foamy waves. His tail is tiny in the distance, so that you get the sense that this is one huge whale.

I worked on shading the water, then the figures. I drew dark clouds gathering—and even managed to make the smudge-smear look dramatic. I gave Jonah dark hair, almost black, whipping behind him in the wind as the boat barrels toward the whale. You couldn't see his face, so you don't know if he's scared, or excited, or worried, or what—which I liked.

I wasn't really happy with the perspective on the boat, but it was getting there, when I smelled roses and bug spray and a moment later someone said, "Wow, Mieka."

Looking up, I saw Jewel standing over me, gazing at my drawing, her lips curved into a smile. Jewel had a beautiful face and with her long curls falling around her, I thought she looked like an angel. A slightly punk angel. That would be another good illustration, I thought, if I could draw her like that.

Carefully, Jewel picked up my picture and held it up for the other campers to see. She didn't say anything, just held it like that, and a murmur rippled through the arts shack.

"Wow!" Shaz stood up to get a closer look. "That's *so* awesome!"

Peter's eyebrows were halfway up his forehead, like he was seriously impressed. My whole body felt like it was glowing warm, in spite of the fact that the arts shack was one of the only buildings at Camp Franklin that had air-conditioning.

"Mieka," Greta said breathlessly, "you're so good! I can't draw at all."

"That's not true," Jewel said, putting my picture down in front of me. "I love how you've drawn the elephants," she gestured gracefully, her finger skimming the air just above Greta's gaudy picture, "with their trunks intertwined."

Actually, Jewel had just picked out the one cute thing in Greta's picture, which was, overall, nothing special. I looked around at the other campers' artwork, and realized that Greta was telling the truth. My picture really was good. I was used to comparing my artwork to my dad's.

"And I love the vibrant colors," Jewel told Greta.

"It's nothing compared to Mieka's," Greta said.

"Art is not a competition," Jewel said, and even

though I knew she was right, I felt a wave of pride wash through me.

Maybe this was what those Persian artists were worried about, I thought. But I decided to just enjoy it. It sure beat getting your butt stuck in a swing.

"Okay, Group Ten!" Ellie announced the next morning. Campers streamed past us, on their way from chapel to their first activities. Pastor Mike had talked about forgiveness, and how important it was. How Jesus even forgave the people who killed him, just like he forgave the whole world for being such a messed-up place. My brain was still whirling from that. I mean, I could barely forgive Tricky for dumping me to hang out with my worst enemy. Then again, I'm not Jesus.

"Group Nine, you too!" Charlie called. "We've got another challenge!"

The other campers let out a whoop and gathered around. Shaz and Peter high-fived. I tried to blend in. Whoopee. Pinch me, before I die of joy.

"We're having a swim race. Relay—we've got to get everyone in each group from one end of the pool to the other In less than fifteen minutes!"

"Oh, thank goodness!" Julie said. Meg and Roxie high-fived. Swimming. Usually, this would have been great news. It was ninety-eight degrees out—boiling.

But not for me. Not today.

As the other girls raced toward the pool's changing room, I skulked over to Ellie. "Uh—Ellie, I don't think I can do the challenge," I said. "I'm not feeling well." I did my best to look like I might fall over at any moment.

She folded her arms across her chest. "What's wrong?"

I looked up at her even features and swallowed a wince. The look on her face said that she doubted I was sick. The doubt made my mouth go dry. I felt like I had just licked the dust from the main camp road.

"Do you need to go to the nurse?" Ellie asked.

"No, but—"

"A cool dip is just what you need." She gave my shoulder a gentle shove, but I rooted my feet into the ground.

"Really, I don't think I—"

"Mieka, is this because of the last challenge?" Ellie asked. "Do you want to talk about it?"

"It's not because of that," I said, but I could tell that she didn't believe me. Still, I didn't know how to explain the truth . . . not to Ellie, anyway. Her perfect skin glowed pink in the hot sun, and her green eyes beamed down at me. Maybe I was just imagining that she thought I was the worst camper in the group. I *hoped* I was just imagining it.

This is bad, I thought as I trudged into the changing room. The smell of chlorine bit into my nostrils as I sat down on the bench. Very bad.

"You okay?" Greta asked.

I looked into her open face. I really did not know what to do, and I needed some help. "I'm getting my period," I whispered in her ear.

Greta's blue eyes went wide. "Oh, no," she said.

"Yeah."

I waited. Greta didn't say anything, and I knew that she hadn't gotten hers yet. Crud. None of my friends at home had gotten it, either. It had only shown up twice before, and never at a time I could predict.

"What are you going to do?" Greta asked.

"Fake my own death?" I suggested.

"You could just sit out," Greta said.

"And tell Ellie, Charlie, and Hunky Greg that I'm on the rag?" I asked. Hunky Greg was our swim counselor. If he found out, I'd die. I'd die, and then I'd die all over again. "Look, I just don't want people to know about this, okay?" Especially Group Nine, I did not need to add. Especially not Peter.

Greta nodded, and made a little gesture like she was locking her lips. I guess we looked like we were whispering about something exciting, because Kristin tiptoed over. "What's wrong?"

"Mieka's getting her period," Greta announced.

"Jeez, Greta! What did I just say?"

"But telling Kristin doesn't count." Greta looked baffled.

"Oh, wow." Kristin thought for a moment. "Can't you use a tampon, or something? I think that's what my mom does."

"Oh, ew," I told her. I'd never used a tampon, and I had no intention of starting today. They were scary.

Julie walked over in her electric blue swimsuit. "What's up?"

"Meeks's cousin Fred is visiting," Kristin replied.

"Lucky," Julie said.

I let out an involuntary groan.

"Why don't you call your mom?" Kristin suggested.

I hesitated for a moment. "I don't have her number memorized," I said finally. This was true, by the way. Of course, the fact that I didn't have her number at all was *more* true, but it wasn't something I wanted to tell Kristin.

Kristin's eyebrows disappeared behind her bangs. "Isn't it your own phone number?"

"She's at work," I pointed out. Again—this was true. As far as I knew. At work in California . . . doing something.

"Isn't she in Houston?" Kristin pressed.

Jeez, what is this? I wanted to ask. Am I on some kind of TV cop show?

But Greta just ignored the question. "Okay, we'll call my mom," she said reasonably. But I really didn't want to talk to Aunt Kate about this. She'd probably give me some "now you're a woman" speech and make me a T-shirt that read, "I'm menstruating!"

"I don't—" But Greta had already dug her cell phone out of her bag and punched the speed dial.

She handed the phone to me, and I had to resist the urge to chuck it across the dressing room.

"What's going on?" Roxie asked.

"Do you mind?" Julie shot back, turning her body to block Roxie's view. "We're having a private conversation."

Roxie retreated, muttering that some people thought they could just boss others around.

Just then, a voice answered—but it wasn't my aunt's. "Hello?" Dad said.

I covered the mouthpiece with my hand. "I thought you called her cell phone!" I hissed at Greta.

"I did!"

"Hello? Hello?"

My dad sounded so lost and small on the other end of the line that I said, "Hi, Dad."

"Mieka! Everything okay?"

"Uh—yeah. Actually, I meant to call Aunt Kate. I thought this was her number."

"It is," Dad said. "She left her cell phone at home. When I saw that it was Greta's number calling, I got worried."

"Oh—right." I put my hand over the mouthpiece again. "Your mom left her phone at home."

"Ask your dad," Greta said.

"No way!"

Julie and Kristen grimaced, like they didn't have a better idea.

"Girls, hurry up in there!" Ellie called. "I want you out here in three minutes!"

"It's just your dad," Greta insisted. "He changed your diapers."

"This is different," I said, and it was, even though I wasn't sure why. "He won't know what to do, anyway."

"He might," Julie said.

"Mieka? You still there?"

"Yeah, Dad. I'm here. Um, everything's okay. . . ."

Ask him, Greta mouthed.

No way, I mouthed back. "Just wanted to say hi! Gotta go!" And I clicked off without another word.

"Now what?" Julie asked.

Greta made a sucking sound with her teeth. "Well, uh—can't you—can't you put a pad in your swimsuit?" she asked after a moment.

Oh, jeez. I rolled my eyes.

"Well, maybe that's not such a bad idea," Julie said.

"I don't know," Kristin said doubtfully. "Won't you be able to see it?"

"Try it," Greta urged, handing me my bathing suit.

"Try it, and if you can see it, we'll tell Hunky Greg that you fainted, or something."

At the thought of facing Hunky Greg and having him know all, I decided I didn't have much of a choice. Quickly, I bought a pad from the dispenser and ducked into one of the toilet stalls. I carefully unwrapped the pad and stuck it into the crotch of my bathing suit, then peeled off my sweaty shirt and shorts and stepped into the one-piece.

I stepped out of the stall and turned around for the Pretties' inspection. "Am I okay?"

"You can't see it," Greta said.

"Not at all," Kristin assured me.

Julie nodded. "You're good."

I breathed a sigh of relief. Okay, water, I thought. Ready or not, here I come.

"Tenners! Let's go!" Ellie shouted, and we all grabbed our towels and scrambled out to the pool. I tried to walk with my thighs together, but then I thought I might be drawing extra attention to myself, so I held my towel in front of me. Peter stood at the edge of the pool, on the other side of the diving board, chatting with Shaz. So far, he hadn't even looked in my direction.

For once, I wanted to keep it that way.

I don't know a lot about praying, but I do know about begging, so I decided I'd give it a try. *Please, God*, I thought, *pleasepleasepleaseplease don't let me humiliate myself again. Yours truly, Mieka.*

"Everyone at the deep end!" Hunky Greg commanded, so we all lined up. Meg was first, then Tanner, Roxie, Kristin, me, Julie, Greta, and Kelli. Kelli went last because she was the strongest swimmer. Hopefully, if we were running behind, she could make up any time we had lost. The boys lined up, too. Peter was their last swimmer, right behind a boy named Kevin. I caught Peter looking in my direction, and I quickly looked away.

And God, if it's not too much trouble, please consider making me invisible.

"Okay, Tenners!" Ellie looked down at her clipboard. "Listen up, Niners, this goes for you, too. We've got fourteen minutes to get everyone to the shallow end and back. So swim your fastest stroke. The next person should dive in the second the person before touches the wall. Meg and Shaz on your mark, get set—" Ellie blew the whistle, and Meg sliced into the water with a perfect shallow dive. Then her arms came up and she blasted through the water with a splashy forward crawl. Around me, Group Ten cheered and whooped. My mouth was so dry that I could barely manage a feeble whistle. I had the worst team spirit of anyone in the cabin, except for Tanner, who never said anything at all.

I shifted my weight nervously from one foot to the other as I watched Julie take off for the far side of the pool. What if my pad falls out while I'm kicking? I thought. Stop thinking that! I commanded myself. That's not going to happen!

But my mind gleefully supplied the mental image of the pad flopping out of my suit and bobbing around the pool like a child's lost water wing. Maybe Shaz would swim right into it. . . .

Just keep your legs together as you kick, I thought.

Kristin was cruising toward our wall in a warped diagonal line, and I crouched into a diving pose, fighting the urge to grab Greta and shove her in line in front of me. *Please, Lord*, I thought, *help*.

And then Kristin's fingers brushed the wall, and I didn't think, I just arced toward the water and then it was cool, such a relief from the fierce sun, and I started to kick and that was when I realized what a horrible mistake I'd made.

I was moving forward, but the crotch of my bathing suit had been left behind, somewhere near my knees. Of course, that pad was designed to be superabsorbent. It had just sucked up half of the pool water and lay like a brick in my swimsuit.

But I couldn't—I *wouldn't*—be the one who blew the team challenge again. No way. So I clamped my thighs together and kicked from the knee, putting all of my energy into pulling myself forward with my arms. I could feel Michael pulling past me on my left, and I wondered if I was swimming too slowly. My triceps ached with the effort, but I made it to the shallow end, tucked into a roll, and pushed off the wall, back toward the deep end. The force sent my pad hurtling dangerously toward my knees, but I kicked and I pulled and I concentrated on breathing at every other stroke, and after a moment, I was reaching out and then I was touching the far wall, and I saw Julie's shadow pass over me, and I yanked off my goggles and that was it. Done. Finito.

"Six minutes, six seconds!" Hunky Greg announced.

"Great job!" Charlie cheered.

I'd made it back in less than two minutes. My arm muscles were sore, but it was okay. I didn't care. I made it in time, I thought as I watched Julie turn the wall. That's all that matters.

"Out!" Hunky Greg shouted at me.

"Mieka, you need to get out of the way!" Ellie called.

But I couldn't get out of the pool. Everyone would see the brick in my crotch. And Peter was standing right at the edge of the pool, next in line. His eyebrows were tucked together, like they wanted to touch. I looked over at my cousin, panicked. And I don't know how she did it, but Greta read my face, and before I could even say anything, she tossed me a towel . . . right into the pool.

"What are you doing?" Greg cried, but I had already grabbed the wet towel. I bobbed over to the silver ladder, wrapped the clinging, sodden ten pounds of terry cloth around my waist, and got out of the pool. I didn't look back as I hurried toward the changing room. There was nothing they could say that would make me stop.

That's the thing about Greta, I thought as I walked into the cool silence of the dressing room and dropped the towel onto the floor with a wet splat. You could pretty much count on her to come up with the stupidest brilliant idea possible.

chapter nine

"*I* think I'm going to take a shower," Greta said later that afternoon as she pecked at her computer keyboard. "I feel like I'm covered in grime after that softball game."

Greta, naturally, didn't look grimy or sweaty or anything. Her hair was still pulled back in a perfect, glossy ponytail. I, on the other hand, looked and felt disgusting. My new pink tank top from Macy's was sweaty and had a huge dirt smear across the front. A shower sounded good to me, too. I decided I'd take one after Greta. "Too bad we don't go to genius camp, like Mark," I said, flopping against the bed pillows. "Then we'd never have to get sweaty."

"Hm." Greta clicked the mouse and shoved her chair

away from the desk. She hummed a little tune as she grabbed some fresh clothes out of her bureau and walked toward the door. But when she reached it, she paused. "You don't need to check your e-mail or anything, do you?" she asked suddenly. She flashed the computer a doubtful look, like it might not want to work for me.

"Not really," I said, putting down the magazine I had been reading and picking another off the side table.

"Okay." Greta hesitated another minute, then left for her shower.

I flipped through the glossy pages. Greta had stacks of them—it looked like she had a subscription to every teen magazine on the planet. Dad makes me buy that kind of stuff with my own money, so we never really have them around the house. "They just make you want stuff you can't afford," he always says. Which, as I stared at the beautiful girl in the dark jeans with a ton of cool jewels in her hair, I realized was true. I'd never really noticed how scruffy my own jeans were. And my shoes—all I had were sneakers. The model was wearing hot-pink flats . . . and I wanted them.

I had all of these new clothes, and I wanted more.

Sighing, I tossed the magazine onto the foot of the

bed and stood up. I wished I had something good to read—like a card from Nana. I hadn't received a post-card from her in the past few days. I decided to check my e-mail, just in case.

I sat down in Greta's stiff-backed chair and swept the mouse across the pad. The screen was filled with purple bubbles. In the lower corner was a small box—the IM chat Greta had been having just a moment before. And I swear that I never would have even glanced at it, normally. But have you ever noticed how your name just jumps off the page at you when you read something? Well, there was my name, right there in the lower-right corner. It wasn't in bold letters, but it might as well have been.

Goldngrl: <urgh! so embarassng>

Gr8a: <nobody saw>

Goldngrl: <still! Mieka looked like a head case running off with your towel>

Gr8a: <I couldn't think of anything else>

Goldngrl: <y couldn't she call her mom? so weird>

Gr8a: <it's just her and her dad. Meek's mom is dead>

Goldngrl: <omg!!!!!!! Y didn't u tell us?>

There was more, but I didn't read it. My eyes were glued to the chat. Meek's mom is dead. Dead.

But that wasn't true.

My mother was in California.

I remembered the day she left. It was January, and freezing in the usual Boston way. Snowflakes tumbled through the air, stinging my eyes. Old, crumbly snow mixed with salt crunched under my feet as I hurried home from school. Mom had told me that she would be gone before I got home, but I wanted to catch her.

The door to our apartment building stood open, and three men were loading our couch into the back of a grimy truck with red lettering. I was surprised by that—I hadn't realized that Mom was taking some of our furniture with her—but, mostly, I was happy that I would get to see her one more time before she left. She wasn't moving to California then, just across town, and I was supposed to have dinner with her over the weekend. Still, I wanted to see her one last time.

I raced up the stairs and down the hall on the third floor. Again, the door was open and Mom was standing in the living room, wearing her heavy coat. The room looked strange—bleak in the dim January light, and nearly empty. Our two brown leather chairs were still there, but the couch was gone, and so was the television set. Other things were missing, too—the paintings that used to hang over our dining room table, the silver lamp, the collection of wooden bowls that sat on the shelves that lined the far wall. Half of the books. It was strange to look around and realize which things had been my mother's favorites, because they were gone.

My mother had her back toward me. Her curly black hair floated over the deep red of her coat and I stood still for a minute, looking at her silhouetted against the windows. She was like a statue, and I knew that in a moment, she would disappear, too.

I was about to say something, but my father walked in from the kitchen and saw me. I barely had time to register how ancient and tired he looked before he said "Mieka" and my mother whirled to face me.

Her mouth hung open a little. She looked sick, and I realized that I had made a mistake in rushing home. A horrible mistake. She didn't want to see me. She just wanted to leave.

"I wanted to say good-bye." I started crying. Not loud and snuffly. Quiet tears streamed down my face, that's all. I couldn't help it.

"Oh, Mieka," my mother said, wrapping me in a hug.

I wanted to stay like that forever, but she pulled away from me and placed her hands at my cheeks. Her nose was practically touching mine, and I got to see her large brown eyes close up. They were lighter toward the center, almost red-brown, and warm. Her black eyeliner was smeared on one side and completely worn off on the other. I wondered if she had been crying and if her chest ached as much as mine did. "I love you," she said.

"I love you, too."

She stood up, and my father put his hand on my shoulder and then she left.

She lived in Newton for a few months. That's a suburb of Boston. It wasn't bad. She had a tiny apartment with bars on the windows and peeling paint, but she made it seem pretty with lots of plants, and paintings on the walls. I would go to visit her on weekends. But then she got a job opportunity in California. Mom told me that she couldn't pass it up. She knew my dad would take good care of me. And she couldn't live her Boston life anymore. That was how she put it. "Her Boston life." She was gone by the end of the summer.

When I thought about it later, I realized that Mom hadn't been herself for weeks before she moved out. Maybe longer. She had been quiet. Thoughtful. She never laughed. She forgot things, left her keys at the supermarket, picked me up from Laurie Cox's party two hours late. But she and my dad never fought, at least not in front of me. The apartment grew silent, and then she left.

So that was it. My mother was in California, not dead. And Greta knew it. She had to, because Aunt Kate came for a visit that summer that Mom moved.

But why had Greta lied? Because she didn't want her friends to know that my mom just took off?

Anger burned through my toes, up my legs, down my arms, into my fingertips. My life was too embarrassing for Greta, so she'd made up a new one for me. Greta told Kristin the one thing that she couldn't freak out about without looking like a total loser. No matter how weird she thought I was, she would still have to be nice to me. Because now I was an orphan. A half-orphan with a tragic past.

Isn't it amazing how Greta always knows what to say? I thought bitterly.

"What's for dinner?" Grandma asked as Aunt Kate slipped a slice of lasagna onto her plate.

"It's vegetarian lasagna, Mother."

"I *mean*," Grandma said as she speared her noodles, "what *else* is for dinner?"

"There's a bowl of salad right in front of you," Dad said. "This is delicious, Katie."

"How do you like it, Mark?" Aunt Kate asked.

Mark gave her a huge spinachy grin. That was an unfair question—that kid eats anything.

Grandma looked exasperated. "Is this what you people call dinner? Where's the food?"

"This is a very healthy dinner," Aunt Kate pointed out.

"Healthy?" Grandma gazed at the lasagna in horror. "There's no protein. You should have put some meat on here."

"Cheese has protein."

"Cheese doesn't have any protein," Grandma insisted. "You need to have meat."

"Oh, Mother, yes it does."

"It does, Mom," Dad agreed.

"I think it does," Greta piped up.

"What do you know?" Grandma's blue eyes dug into Greta's face like talons. My cousin shrank under the stare.

I should say something, I thought. I happened to know for a fact that cheese has protein. I mean, everyone knows that. But I decided to keep my mouth shut. Finally, something embarrassing happened to Miss Perfect. Not as embarrassing as what happened to me, but at least now she knows how it feels. Besides, it wouldn't do any good. There's no way to change Grandma's mind about something, no matter how wrong it is.

"You should try to eat more healthfully, Mother," Aunt Kate said. "It'll cut your risk of having another heart attack."

"If you were so worried about me," Grandma snapped, "you'd give me something decent to eat during my final days on this earth."

"So, where's Dave?" Dad asked. His voice was way too loud, and it was obvious that he was just changing the subject.

"At work," my aunt said with a sigh.

"You should be glad to have a hardworking man," Grandma scolded. "Your father never worked a day in his life."

Dad looked like he'd been socked in the gut. "That's not true!"

"It is," Grandma shot back.

"He worked until the day he died," Dad insisted.

Grandma snorted. "If that's the story, then I guess you can believe it."

Dad looked like he wanted to say more, but Mark cut him off. "Mieka, will you read to me after supper?" he asked.

"Sure," I said.

"That's boring," Greta piped up. "Let's play Twister."

"I hate Twister," I said, staring at my plate. I didn't actually hate Twister—I just didn't want to agree with anything Greta said ever again.

"Twister is fun!" Greta insisted.

"'Oh, how long will you simple ones love your

simple ways?'" I asked with a sigh.

"What?" Greta asked, but I knew that she'd heard me. It was what Pastor Mike had said yesterday. He'd been talking about challenging ourselves, blah, blah, blah, and he had quoted from the Bible.

"I think I'd rather do something that uses my mind, thanks," I snapped, looking Greta in the face. "But if you want to play Twister, go ahead."

"It's good that somebody's got some brains around here," Grandma grumbled.

"Mother," Aunt Kate said.

"What? I'm just saying that Greta isn't going to win any national spelling bees, that's all," Grandma insisted. "It's not like it's a secret. Mieka's just telling it like it is."

"I'll play Twister with you, Greta," Mark volunteered. "We can do both."

Greta tried to smile at her little brother, but it wobbled. "That's okay," she said. Her voice was lower than usual, almost husky. "You just play with Mieka."

"Nobody wants to tell the truth around here," Grandma muttered. Her bird glance fell on me, and she gave me an almost-smile. As if she was glad I'd hurt Greta's feelings.

I didn't know what to make of it. It made me proud and ashamed all at once.

chapter ten

"What's the occasion?" I asked my dad as he walked into the kitchen.

It was early, and I was the first one awake, as usual. I'd poured myself a bowl of rice cereal, which was crackling in the lake of milk beneath it. Still an hour and fifteen minutes before Aunt Kate had to take us to camp, which was fine with me. I like being awake in a sleepy house. I like hearing people get up, watching the sunrise, getting dressed slowly.

"Breakfast meeting," my dad said throatily, his eyes still half-slits. Then he added, "Don't look at me like that."

"Like what?" I asked.

"Like 'how in the world can *you* have a breakfast meeting?'" Dad said as he made his way to the freezer and pulled out an orange-and-white bag of coffee.

"Well, how can you?" I asked.

"Hey there, Jeff-O!" Uncle Dave bellowed as he strode into the room. "Lookin' mighty sharp!"

It took me a minute to process what my uncle had just said, but once the words sank into my brain, I realized that he was right. My dad was wearing pressed khaki pants and a blue-and-white, short-sleeved button-down shirt. He even had on shiny black slip-on shoes and—get this—a matching leather belt.

"What's going on?" I asked, thinking, What happened to the paint-splattered sweats?

"You inspired me," Dad said. "I thought I deserved some new clothes, too."

"Really?" I asked.

Dad smiled. "Sort of."

Uncle Dave laughed as Dad measured out the coffee. "Didn't your dad tell you? He's going to help us with some of our Web design."

"Just contract work," Dad put in quickly.

"For now." Uncle Dave clapped him on the back.

"Oh." I took another spoonful of my noisy cereal, thinking. My dad actually knew a lot about Web design—he'd set up his own site to sell his artwork, and had helped out a lot of his friends with their designs. But that had always been for fun. He was an artist, not a Web designer.

"Don't drink too much of that coffee," Uncle Dave teased Dad as he poured the dark liquid into a mug. Coffee is a weird thing—it smells good and tastes terrible. I don't understand how people can drink it. I mean, how can they live with that kind of daily disappointment?

"If I don't have my coffee, I won't be able to get my eyes open," Dad told my uncle.

"That's true," I confirmed.

Uncle Dave laughed like I'd said the funniest thing in the universe, then tromped out of the kitchen saying, "We need to leave in ten minutes, Jeff-O."

"I'll be ready," Dad called as he sank into the pine chair beside mine.

I listened to Uncle Dave's noisy retreat toward the bathroom. It was hard to imagine my dad getting all businessy with his company. "Dad . . . ?"

"Yeah?" His gray eyebrows twitched upward slightly.

I wanted to tell him about Greta—how she'd lied about Mom—but then stopped. It didn't seem like the right time—before his big meeting, and all. "Dad— would you come to Parents' Day?" I asked instead. "It's next Friday."

Dad's coffee mug hesitated at the edge of his lip. Finally, he took a sip, then asked, "At Camp Franklin?"

"Yeah."

Dad sighed. He's slow in the morning—moves slow, thinks slow. I could tell that the thought was buzzing around in his mind, like a heavy bumblebee. "I don't know, Mieka."

I didn't say anything. I just looked at him.

"You really want me to?" he asked.

"Yeah," I said.

Nodding, Dad took another sip of his coffee, then turned to stand up just as Grandma shuffled into the kitchen.

"What's everyone doing up?" she growled. A grimace flashed across her gray face as she lowered herself slowly into the chair across from mine.

"Dad's got a business meeting," I told her.

"Really." It wasn't a question. She sat back in her chair and gave Dad a droopy look. "Is that why he looks so spiffy?"

The word "spiffy" made me snort a little, and I choked on a piece of cereal. Dad looked so surprised that I laughed harder.

Grandma looked at me sharply, a tiny smile curling at the corner of her mouth. "Should we declare it a national holiday?" she asked.

"I've got to get going." Ignoring her last comment, Dad took his half-empty mug to the sink. The bottom tipped slightly against the lip of the counter. "Crap!" he cried as a hot splash landed on his thigh. "I don't have any other pants."

"Coffee isn't hard to get out," I said quickly. "Just put water on it."

"It won't dry!" Dad cried. "I can't go to a meeting with wet pants!"

"Use a hair dryer."

Dad's blue eyes focused on me. "Really? Does that work?" he asked, like he couldn't believe that I had this incredible secret knowledge.

I shrugged. "I spill a lot of stuff on myself," I told him.

Grandma picked a dead leaf off the small ivy plant at the center of the table. "Who knew that would come in handy?" she asked. But it didn't have her usual edge. She looked worn out, like the rag Dad keeps draped over the neck of our kitchen faucet. I guessed maybe she was too tired to be mean.

Dad paused to look at me. He touched my hair—just a featherweight of fingers at the crown of my head—then hurried down the hall.

Grandma didn't say a word and neither did I as I rinsed my bowl in the sink and put it in the dishwasher. I wished she were Nana, so that I could tell her what Greta had done. But I didn't trust Grandma. I was mad at Greta—but not *that* mad.

"Okay, everyone," Jewel said, "visualize the object you will create."

I stared at the hunk of clay on the table in front of me. I visualized a hunk of clay.

"You have to see it before you can create it."

Greta was sitting on the other side of the arts shack, tucked into a corner beside Julie. She hadn't said any thing to me all day.

I hadn't said anything to her, either.

It was weird—we hadn't officially fought. We just weren't talking. I didn't know if we'd ever speak to each other again. I knew one thing, though—I was done trying to be Greta. Being Greta meant being fake.

"This clay can be anything you want," Jewel went on. "Anything at all. You can make a coil bowl. Or you can make a sculpture, an animal, a dish . . ."

"An ashtray," Meg muttered from the seat next to me.

That made me laugh a little.

Shaz raised his hand in the air. "I'm done," he said.

Jewel looked at the blob in front of him. "You haven't even started yet."

"You said it could be anything," Shaz protested, his brown eyes huge. The rest of his table—Peter, Mark, and Jake—cracked up.

The look Jewel gave him was actually painful to witness, and Shaz immediately bent over his clay and started rolling it into a long snake. The truth was that I had been tempted to say the same thing—until that moment. Jewel looked like a peace-and-love hippie chick, but she had some steel in her, too.

I looked at my clay, hoping that it would inspire me,

but all it did was remind me of the cereal I'd eaten for breakfast. It had been as lumpy as the clay. I thought about my dad and his blank canvas. He still couldn't make the dragon look right. He'd told me the other night that he was afraid he was losing his talent. He'd looked so frightened that he'd actually frightened me a little.

"Don't let it pressure you," Jewel said as she slid into the chair across from me.

"Pressure me?"

"The clay." Jewel looked at it, pursing her lips. "Remember that you're the boss, not it."

"Okay," I said.

"Seen anything cool in clay lately?" Jewel asked.

"No," I told her. Then I remembered a postcard Nana had sent me recently. It was from a museum, and it had a picture of a clay bowl on the front. Some sort of ancient pottery. It was really plain, just a round brown bowl with a tiny hole at the top. But it was something like five thousand years old, from Iran. "Wait, yes," I corrected myself. I briefly explained the bowl.

"It was Persian," Jewel told me. "That's where the art of pottery began. They also made little animals and decorative things. Cool flasks for wine that looked like camels."

What's with Jewel and the Persians? I wondered as I touched the clay. It was dense and surprisingly cool under my fingers. First the Persian Flaw, and now this. "Don't you need a wheel to make a bowl like that?" I was thinking about a potter I'd seen on TV. Brown clay poured over her fingers like melted chocolate. She bent over her wheel as it spun, spun, spun, turning out a tall, slim, perfectly round vase.

"They didn't have wheels in ancient Persia," Jewel told me. "They did it all by hand."

"Really?" I imagined the kind of bowl I'd like to make—small and poufy, like a closed-up sea anemone, with sides that curved gracefully. My lump of clay didn't look anything like that.

"It just takes a long time," Jewel said. "You have to be patient." And then she nodded and moved on to the next art victim.

Picking up the clay, I rolled it between my two hands. It was heavy, so I soon switched to rolling it against the table. Then I put my index finger in the center. It sank down, and the clay sucked and clung as I pulled it back out. But I put my finger in again and wiggled it around, making the center hole larger. Then I took my left hand and pressed against the outer wall as I pushed out from the inside.

The wall of my bowl was lumpy, and I worked to smooth it so that it curved in evenly. It was harder than I thought it would be. The minute I got one part smoothed, I'd move on to the next and manage to put a dent in the bit I'd just finished.

If I had a wheel, I thought, this would look perfect. But I didn't have a potter's wheel. Besides, I didn't know how to use one. It seemed really easy when I saw it on TV, but something told me that it was harder than it looked.

Nana said on her postcard that the jug pictured on the front was huge, like three feet high. How long had it taken to make it? I wondered. I pictured an ancient Iranian artisan slaving away over this giant jug, and felt sorry for her. I wondered if she would have felt better knowing that it had lasted for five thousand years, and that it was in a museum, where people bought postcards with pictures of it on the front that they mailed to their granddaughters.

I was about halfway finished when Jewel said, "Okay, campers, time to get to the sing."

What? Looking around, I realized that everyone else was cleaning up. A table at the front of the shack was covered with clay objects—a cat, a mug made of a long curled snake of clay (Shaz's, I bet), and a bunch of things that could have been anything.

Greta's blue eyes caught mine for a moment, then flashed away. Her expression was strange—not angry, exactly. Sad, maybe?

I had this sudden feeling, like if I had to leave the arts shack, I'd die. I can't explain it. My throat closed, and I knew that if anyone tried to force me to sing, I'd asphyxiate and keel over. Then the camp would be liable for my death.

"Jewel?" I asked. "Can I stay?"

Jewel looked surprised, like nobody had ever asked to do extra arts and crafts before.

I pointed to my bowl. "I'm almost done," I told her, which was a bit of an exaggeration, but kind of true.

"She just wants to stay in the air-conditioning," Kelli said.

"Ooh, yeah, I want to stay, too!" Shaz put in. "I just

remembered that I need to do more work on my project!"

Peter punched him in the arm and smiled at me. Any other time, my heart would have melted—but I guess I was just too overwhelmed to swoon.

Ignoring their comments, Jewel gathered her mane of dark blond hair behind her head and tied it into a knot. She looked thoughtfully at my bowl. "Okay," she said after a moment. "I have to stick around and clean up, anyway."

"What?" Roxie cried. "Hey, that's not fair!"

"I'll see you girls on Thursday," Jewel said, ushering Roxie, Kelli, and Meg out the door. "Bye-bye! Have fun at the sing."

Roxie glared at me, and I gave her a bright little buh-bye! wave and a smile. Hah. I really did want to stay and finish my bowl, but the air-conditioning was a definite bonus.

Once the Niners and Tenners had stampeded through the door, Jewel turned on some music and started to sort through the clay sculptures, placing them on a nearby shelf. Then she moved on to the paintbrushes—making sure that they were organized by size. I watched her from under my eyelashes for a while, and then I got to work.

The wall on one side was much thicker than the wall on the other, so I set to work evening it out. Once that was finished, I worked to make the shape symmetrical. That was a pain. Each time I thought I had it, I noticed that there was a piece that looked a little off. Then I'd work on that piece, and another part would be off. I kept the image of the sea anemone in my mind, and worked and worked.

Finally, finally, I felt a gentle hand on my shoulder. "It's beautiful, Mieka," Jewel said.

"It is?" I stared at the bowl. It was plain, but all of my fussing had actually paid off—it was even and looked almost exactly the way I had imagined. It was about the size of my hand, fingers outstretched, small and plain.

"Should I put a pattern around the edge, or something?"

"Leave it," Jewel said. "Simplicity is the hardest thing. Besides, you have to get to your afternoon activity."

"What?" I looked at my watch. Sure enough, I'd worked straight through the sing *and* lunch.

"It's easy to lose yourself when you're making something," Jewel said. "When you're focused on something in front of you, you can lose time, lose thoughts."

I nodded. Dad had told me that once—when he painted, it was like the rest of the world stopped. Sometimes, when I interrupted him, he'd blink at me, like he was trying to remember who I was, what I was doing there.

Carefully, like she was cradling a kitten, Jewel lifted the bowl and carried it over to the shelf to dry. It sat squat and small among the other pieces, huddled with them like a friend.

At that moment, I heard the thud of footsteps on the stairs outside. The door to the arts shack burst open with a bang, and there was Greta—her blond bangs clinging to her sweaty forehead, her blue eyes wide. I was just about to tell her that it was okay, I was on my way to afternoon activity, when I noticed her expression. Once, when Dad and I were driving down the highway, I saw a deer lying in the middle of the road. It had been hit by a car, but it wasn't dead. It lifted its head in pain and confusion, its eyes blank. That was how Greta looked right now.

"Are you all right?" Jewel asked.

Greta and I aren't speaking to each other, I thought. So why is she here?

"Mieka," she gasped, and I knew.

"Want to play again?" Mark asked, kicking his feet out from the plush navy blue chair. We were sitting in a waiting area, but it wasn't like what you see on TV. It was a large atrium filled with plants and comfortable chairs. The walls were hung with brightly colored children's paintings. In the corner were several vending machines, which Mark had been eyeing since we arrived, three hours before. "I'm hungry," he whined, and when he got a bag of Cheetos, he announced that he was thirsty, too. When that was finished, he was hungry again. Personally, I think he just liked feeding the money into the machine.

Mark pointed a chubby finger at the deck of cards on the low pine table between our chairs. "Just one more," he begged. "Please?"

"Not right now," I told him. We had just played seventeen games of War in a row. I couldn't take any more. Greta was asleep in the chair beside mine. At least she looked like she was asleep . . . but part of me wondered if she was just faking it, so that she wouldn't have to play cards with her little brother.

"What did the nurses say?" Dad asked as Aunt Kate appeared.

"They're not out of surgery yet," she said, flopping into the chair across from Mark's. "They'll let us know as soon as they hear anything." Aunt Kate twisted her mouth and raised her eyebrows, as though she had heard that line a thousand times. Which maybe she had, given that she kept getting up to go to the nurses' station. "I never should have let her smoke in the house." She shook her head. "I should have known this would happen."

"She should have known it," Dad snapped. "If she doesn't want to take care of herself, what can we do about it?" He slammed the magazine he had been reading onto the table in front of him. "I'm going for a walk," he announced.

"Mieka, can we play a game?" Mark asked.

Oh, lord, not another game. "Can I come?" I asked my dad.

My dad hesitated a moment, like maybe he wanted to

take the walk by himself. Then he said, "Okay," like he was still thinking about it—he drew out the *O*, then ended with a clipped *kay*. I was about to tell him to forget it, to go ahead without me, when he nodded, adding, "Sure," like he really meant it this time, so I decided that it really was fine if I came along.

"Sorry, Mark," I said as I shoved myself out of the chair. "Maybe we can play when I get back."

Shrugging, Mark moved on to his next victim—poking Greta in the shoulder. She griped drowsily and swatted him away as I hurried after my father.

We walked through the long, white corridor, then took an elevator down five stories. I thought that Dad was just going to walk around the halls, but instead he took us to the lobby and walked straight out the front glass doors.

Nights in Houston make you feel like you're underwater. You move through the warm air slowly. I imagined silver bubbles trailing from my mouth toward the inky sky, as Dad and I glided across the ghostly white sidewalk that wound around the edge of the hospital.

My dad blew out a breath, and I slipped my hand into his. I didn't know what to say. I didn't want to tell him that Grandma would be okay, when I wasn't really sure that she would. I *hoped* she would be okay. Even though she was just about the meanest person I'd ever met. Or even *heard* of. Still—I wanted her to be all right.

Dad wrapped his huge fingers around mine. "Are you okay, Mieka?" he asked me.

"Me? I'm fine." I considered the question. "Are *you* okay?"

"I'm worried." Dad looked out over the cars in the parking lot. They were gleaming dully in the light from the lamps overhead.

We walked on, our footsteps falling into a regular rhythm.

"Mieka . . ." Stopping suddenly, Dad turned to face me. He looked so serious that for a moment I thought he was going to tell me that he was sick, or that something had happened to Nana, but what he said was ". . . Mieka, what do you think of Houston? Do you like it?"

What kind of a question is that? I wondered. Do I like Houston? "Sure," I said. "I mean, it's hot now. But I bet it's nice in the winter. And there's lots to do here. It's green, for a city. It's not Boston . . . but it's still nice."

"It's not Boston?" Dad was prompting me.

"Well—you can't walk places or get around on the T," I explained. "You need a car to go everywhere. But people are really friendly here."

Dad seemed to think this over. "What would you think if we moved down here?"

"What?" I was glad that Dad was holding my hand at that moment, because I nearly fell over.

"There's an opening at Uncle Dave's company— they're looking for someone to manage their Web site. The base pay isn't much, but if the site takes off, I could earn a lot of money—"

"What?" I said again. "You—you want to work for Uncle Dave's company?"

Dad dropped my hand and ran his palms over his face. "Well, I could still paint," he said. "On weekends."

He was talking, but the words weren't really penetrating my brain. My dad wanted to do something other than paint? I couldn't really imagine it. I mean, he might as well have told me that he was thinking of becoming a ballerina, or a squirrel, or something. "You're a painter." Even as I said it, an image of his blank canvas popped into my mind.

"I know, and I'll always be a painter," Dad agreed. "But, Mieka, if we had some more money, we could—do things. . . ."

"We do things," I protested.

"We could do more things," Dad said.

"Like what?"

"Well . . ." He cleared his throat, shrugging. "Wouldn't you like to travel?"

"We're traveling right now," I pointed out.

Dad blinked at me. "Mieka, I need to start thinking about your college fund. I need to worry about my retirement. And wouldn't you like to live in a bigger house? With a yard?"

A house with a yard, I thought. I had to admit that it would be nice. And wouldn't it be fun to be able to go into a store and buy whatever I wanted, the way Greta does? Wouldn't it be nice to say good-bye to Arielle and Tricky? I could start over in a new school, without them. That was seriously tempting. On the other hand, I didn't want to leave Nana.

"I don't know," I said finally.

"Well," Dad said slowly, taking my hand again, "think about it, okay?"

Our fingers were interlaced—mine looked small and slender next to his, locked in a tiny round web. I felt a pulse against my palm, and I wasn't sure whether it was his or my own.

chapter eleven

*I*t was late when we got home. Dad dragged Mark's heavy sleeping form out of the car and carried him upstairs, while Greta and I trudged up to her room. And even though the idea of not brushing my teeth made my mouth feel like it was full of fuzz, I just couldn't bring myself to do it. Too tired.

I couldn't pull off my clothes, either. I just flopped on the white eyelet bedspread and tucked the pillow under my head. Across the room, I heard Greta's bed creak as she climbed on top of it.

She hadn't said a word to me since saying my name that afternoon, but I didn't feel like she was angry with me anymore. I just got the feeling that she was too over-whelmed to talk. We all were. First, with fear. Then, once the doctors had come out of surgery and told us that Grandma was stable—that she was resting in the intensive care unit, but that we could speak to her tomorrow—well, by then we were too relieved to do anything but hold each other's hands and trudge home.

It's amazing how falling asleep really feels like falling. I felt the ceiling drop away above me the minute I closed my eyes.

That was when I heard the scratching noise, like a fingernail across an emery board.

At first, I wasn't sure what the noise was—a mouse? A roach? Roaches in Houston, by the way, are about twenty times the size of roaches anywhere else. Oh, and they can fly. Dis-gusting. I tensed, and was just about to give up and assume I'd imagined it, when the noise sounded again. Only this time, I knew what it was—a sniffle.

Great. Greta was crying.

I know, I know, I sound heartless. But it didn't seem fair that I had to deal with this right now. I mean, I was *tired*. And my dad had just handed me this news about maybe moving to Houston. Besides, Grandma was my grandmother, too. I cared about her. But now I felt like a jerk for not crying over her, the way Greta was.

I tried ignoring the snuffles for a few moments, but then I *really* felt like a loser, so finally I said, "Are you okay?" My words sounded bigger and heavier in the darkness, somehow.

Greta was silent for a moment—maybe she'd thought that I was asleep. "I'm fine."

"Are you crying?"

She sniffed. "Yeah," Greta said, "but it's no big deal. Go to sleep."

I shoved the pillow under my chin. "I'm not sleepy," I lied. "Grandma's going to be okay."

"I know." Greta's voice was wobbly, like it might collapse on her. "That's not it."

That's not it? "Then—what?"

"I'm sorry." Her voice whispered across the ghostly white bedspread and floated out into the room. For a moment, I wondered if I had misheard her.

"For what?"

Greta sniffled twice. "For lying about your mom. You weren't supposed to see the screen. You *never* use the computer," she added.

I pressed my face against the soft pillow, feeling the

smooth cotton against my cheek. Until that moment, I hadn't been sure that she knew why I was angry. I was surprised at how relieved I felt, now that she had said something. My voice sounded soft and small as I heard myself ask, "Why did you do it?"

Silence fell like a curtain between us. It lasted so long that for a moment, I wondered if Greta had fallen asleep. But finally, she said, "You don't know what it's like."

"What *what's* like?"

Greta turned her face toward mine. "Kristin and Julie," she said. "I just didn't want them to know the truth. They'd think it was weird, and then . . ."

"Aren't they your friends?" I asked.

"Yes." Greta sighed. "I guess. I don't know."

I thought about that for a moment. "I do know what it's like," I told her.

Silence settled over us again.

"Do you remember when you asked if Kristin was my best friend?" Greta asked.

I had to think a moment. That question seemed so far away—I'd asked it the first day I got to Houston. "Yeah."

"Well, she used to be." I heard Greta sigh, and her sheets rustled slightly as she shifted in her bed.

"What happened?"

"She started spending all of her time with Julie," Greta said. "I guess they're best friends now."

"I thought best friends were forever."

"I thought so, too."

A car hummed past on the quiet street below.

I rolled over onto my side. Moonlight shone in through the window, illuminating Greta's pale hair. "I'm sorry, too," I said finally. She was backlit by the moon, so I couldn't see her eyes, but I could feel her looking at me. "I shouldn't have called you 'simple.' Especially in front of Grandma. Anyway, it's not true."

Greta didn't say anything for a moment, so I guess she was thinking this over. "Did you know that I get straight A's in school?"

"Really?" I was surprised.

"I'm in the Vanguard program," Greta said. "Honors classes, basically."

Now I really felt like a jerk, because the minute that she'd said that she got straight A's, I'd thought—Yeah, well, you're not in honors classes.

"People always assume I'm stupid," Greta went on. "Or—it's more like—they don't care whether I'm smart or not."

"But everyone likes you."

"Grandma hates my guts," Greta pointed out.

"Grandma hates everyone's guts."

"Yeah." Greta sighed. "Anyway, it doesn't mean much if people like you when they don't even know you."

I thought about Cinderella, how the prince fell in love with her on sight. I wondered how it would feel to know that someone loved you because of how you looked instead of because of who you were. As much as it would suck to be Cinderella's stepsister—being Cinderella would suck in its own way, too. "It's probably worse because of Mark," I said.

"What?"

"You know—because he's a genius."

"What are you talking about?" Greta asked. She sounded genuinely confused.

"Well . . ." My voice faltered. Now *I* was confused. Why doesn't Greta know what I'm talking about? I wondered. "Doesn't he . . . you know, go to genius camp?"

"Oh, that." Greta rolled onto her back and stared up at the ceiling. "It's a camp for kids with learning disabilities."

"What?"

"It's for kids who are smart—like Mark. But they all have these . . . challenges. Do you know what dyslexia is?"

"Sure—you mix up letters when you read."

"Yeah."

Wow. I couldn't believe that Aunt Kate had never mentioned that detail about Mark.

Greta sighed. "It must be four in the morning."

"At least." I yawned.

"Good night, Mieka," Greta said.

"Good night." I rolled onto my back and stared up at the ceiling, invisible in the dark room. I waited to feel the sensation of falling, but it didn't come. Instead, I felt stubbornly stuck to the bed, trapped in the present with my cousin.

My cousin, the beautiful honor student who always knew what to say. How on earth can we be related? I wondered.

chapter twelve

"*H*i, Mom!" Aunt Kate chirped as we stepped into the room in the ICU. We walked carefully, like we were climbing into a lifeboat. I'd never seen so many machines in my life. There were three different monitors with beeps moving across, plus tubes taped to her arms and snaking into her nose, and everything was a jumble of wires and noises.

Grandma opened her eyes heavily, as though weights were sitting on her lids. Her skin was gray and saggy— she looked like a pool float missing half of its air. It was amazing to think how different a person could look in a matter of hours. The sight of her—small and shrunken like that—made my chest tight. This was my grandmother . . . my grandmother who didn't like me. And if she died, she'd *never* like me.

She parted her lips and coughed, causing one of the machines to blip. Her head shook slightly, and she tried again.

Dad leaned closer to hear what she had to say.

"Coffee," Grandma gasped.

Nodding, my dad grabbed his mother's hand. "I'll get you some from across the street," he told her. "It's bound to be better than what they've got in the cafeteria here."

"Jeff." Aunt Kate looked at him sharply, cocking her head to the side. "The doctors say no coffee."

"Doctors," Grandma scoffed, her voice a pale gasp.

My dad looked stricken. "You're right," he told my aunt. "Okay. Mom," he leaned over his mother and spoke more slowly, as though he was going to explain something complicated to a kindergartner. "I'm sorry—we can't get you any coffee."

Grandma looked at Dad for a long moment. Then she closed her eyes and turned her face away.

It was like she was shutting him out—shutting him out completely.

I felt Greta turn to face me—her eyes were huge. Reaching out, I wrapped my index finger around hers.

"Is Grandma asleep?" Mark asked, looking up at Aunt Kate.

"She's tired." But Aunt Kate was the one who sounded tired.

"Okay." My father touched Grandma's lank gray hair and leaned back. "I guess you need your rest," he said quietly.

The scene blurred, but I swallowed hard, choking back the tears. I wasn't sad. I was just . . .

So.

Angry.

I wanted to smash the machines, to scream, to pry her eyes open and make her look at Dad.

But I didn't.

Instead, I took a deep breath, then I followed my aunt as we all tiptoed out as quietly as we came in.

"That was . . . interesting," Dad said as we followed the milling parents and kids out of the Sing Pit. Greta and I had skipped four days of camp after Grandma got sick again, but Greta insisted on coming back for Parents' Day. Camp Franklin had started things off as usual—with chapel. We'd done the usual—Pastor Mike told us a story, we watched as some of the younger campers performed a skit about being honest, and then we sang a song. By now, I was so used to the routine that I didn't even spend a single brain cell thinking about it.

"It was?" I asked him. "What part?"

Dad shrugged. "I don't know. That song about the worm."

"The worm?"

"You know—'the worm makes all thing grow,'" Dad sang. "'He's the light, you know.'"

I stared at him, then started to laugh. I couldn't help him. The worm!

"What's so funny?"

"It's 'the *word*,' Dad!" I punched him in the arm. "'He's the *Word*!' It's a song about Jesus!"

"Oh." Dad looked so funny—like a cartoon character with a lightbulb that had just lit up over his head—that I started to giggle again. "Well, I guess that makes more sense."

No wonder I'm a religion reject, I thought. Look who raised me!

I dragged Dad into the arts shack, where a bunch of Niners, Tenners, and parents were milling around. "Isn't this just so fun?" Aunt Kate asked as she walked up to me holding a purple-and-lavender lanyard that Greta had made. "Look at that wall of Bible stories!"

"Mieka did the whale," Greta piped up.

"Really?" Dad asked, sounding impressed. Reaching over, he pulled the picture off the wall and studied it. "This is great, Meeks." Then, more quietly, he added, "Jonah," like he was surprised that he got it.

"Oh, you're taking away my whale?" Jewel wailed jokingly as she hurried over. Her hair had purple streaks today—honestly, she kind of looked like Greta's lanyard—but she had replaced her nose ring with a tiny diamond that was barely visible against her pale skin.

"You can keep it," I told her, "if you really want it."

"Seriously?" Jewel's green eyes lit up. "Are you sure—are you sure your dad doesn't want it?"

"Oh, he doesn't care," I said, but when I looked over at Dad, I saw that he was looking at the picture like he didn't want to let it go. Oops.

"I'll draw you another one," I promised.

Dad smiled, almost like he was embarrassed about his grip on the whale, and handed it over to Jewel, whose face lit up in a grin. "Beautymous! I'll use it to teach perspective."

I took a step toward the table where our pottery was laid out. Jewel had dipped everything into clear glaze, and for a moment, I didn't spot my bowl amid the brown figures.

"Oh, now this is truly gorgeous!" a red-haired woman said.

"That's not mine," Meg told her.

"It's gorgeous, anyway," the woman—her mother, I guess—said, and when I looked where she was pointing, I saw that her finger led right to a small sea anemone—my bowl.

"That really is nice," my father agreed.

Suddenly, I felt too shy to grab the bowl, but I didn't want to leave without it, either. So I just pretended that I hadn't heard the red-haired woman and picked up the bowl.

"You did that?" Dad's eyebrows floated upward.

"It's just gorgeous," Meg's mother told me.

"Mieka's a great artist," Meg said.

I am? I didn't even know Meg. It seemed weird that she could think something like that about me. Weird, but nice. "Thanks, Meg."

Meg shrugged. "It's the truth," she said, like it was no big deal.

"Where should we put this?" Dad asked, holding it up.

I felt a flash of pride at how nicely it had turned out. For a moment, I wanted to say, "On our coffee table," but I stopped myself.

No.

I should give it away, I realized. Pastor Mike's story from that morning echoed through my mind. He had been talking about forgiveness—about how important it was to care about people, even if they don't care about you. At the time, I'd thought about how easy that was to say—and how much harder it was to do. But now, I felt like I should try. "I think I'll give it to Grandma," I said.

"Really?" Surprise flashed across Dad's face, and something else—something I couldn't read. "Are you sure?"

I looked at the bowl more closely. It had come out even better than I had expected. I mean, nobody would mistake it for a something made by a master potter, but it was good. "Yeah, I'm sure," I told him.

"Oh, what a pretty little pot," Aunt Kate said as she walked up to my dad. "Mieka, did you make that?"

"Yep," I told her.

"A chip off the old block," my aunt said, rubbing Dad's shoulder.

Dad smiled proudly at the bowl. "I guess she is."

"We've got twenty minutes until we're supposed to be at the games lawn," Greta said. The counselors had arranged for us to play parent-camper games in the afternoon. "Let's go to the snack shack and get some ice cream."

"As long as it's not strawberry," Dad said, giving me a wink as we walked out of the shack.

"I want to see the archery range," Aunt Kate put in suddenly. "Is it still behind the snack shack? Maybe we can get ice cream and walk over."

"The infamous archery range." My dad chuckled.

"What?" Greta looked up at her mom. "What's so infamous about it?"

"Oh, this kid bet your mom that she couldn't hit the target," Dad explained. "So she nailed the bull's-eye three times in a row."

"Really?" Greta squealed.

Aunt Kate sighed dreamily. "Adam Stanley," she said. "What a jerk he was." She giggled, which made me and Greta crack up.

Julie and Kristin were standing under a huge oak tree with their parents. They looked over when they heard us laughing. Julie gave Greta a little wave, and Greta waved back. But they didn't come over, and Greta didn't hurry over there. We just kept walking.

"This heat is getting to me." Dad slid onto a bench near the snack shack, licking a chocolate drip that was making its way down the side of his sugar cone. "I've been out of Texas too long."

"I haven't," my aunt said, "and it's getting to me, too." She dipped her plastic spoon into her scoop of maple walnut. "Thank goodness for ice cream."

"Mmm-hmm," I agreed, taking a lick of my scoop of strawberry cheesecake. Dad had tried to argue that all forms of strawberry ice cream were off-limits for the summer, but I'd pointed out that the cheesecake made it legal. Greta and Aunt Kate had backed me up, so here I was—in heaven.

"Meeks," Greta said, gesturing to the collar of her shirt. "You've got a little—"

Looking down, I noticed a smear of pink to the right of my chin. "Dang!"

Greta tossed a crumpled-up napkin at my head. "Don't make fun of my accent!"

"I didn't mean to!" Honestly, that word had just come out.

"Mieka's turning Texan," Dad teased.

Aunt Kate smiled. "It's in her genes."

I dabbed at the smudge with my napkin, but it didn't do much good. "I'm going to get a glass of water," I said, hauling myself off the bench. "Be right back."

When I walked up to the counter, Peter was standing there. He had a bag of popcorn in one hand and a fruit smoothie in the other, and he smiled when he saw me.

A chill ran through me, even under the wicked sun. *Please don't notice the pink smear on my shirt*, I begged silently. "Hey."

"Hey, yourself." He nodded at my collar. "Nice strawberry smudge."

I forced myself not to groan. "Yeah—it's a little project I've been working on."

Peter nodded. "You wear it well."

"So—are your parents here?" I picked up the pitcher of ice water on the counter and poured some into a plastic glass. Then I stuck a napkin in the water and dabbed it against my collar.

"I'm hanging with Shaz and his parents." Peter jutted his chin behind me. Turning, I saw Shaz sitting at a picnic table with a bearded man and a dark-skinned, large-eyed woman. "What about you?"

"I'm with my dad and my aunt," I explained, looking over toward our bench.

"Oh, right—I forgot you and Greta were cousins." Peter nodded. "That's cool."

I laughed a little. "Yeah," I said. "It is."

"Your mom couldn't make it?"

For a moment, I considered using the same line I'd used on Kristin and Julie. I could have just said that she was at work. But that felt like a lie. Instead, I heard myself say, "She lives in California. It's just me and my dad."

Peter winced. "Sorry."

I shrugged. "It's okay." I stuffed my smudgy napkin into the plastic cup and tossed them both into the trash. My collar was still slightly pink, but it wasn't as bad as before.

"Really?" Peter looked doubtful.

I thought it over. "No."

"Yeah." Peter took a sip of his smoothie. I expected him to say, "Well, see you later," but instead he said, "Sometimes I wish my parents would get a divorce." He watched me closely as he said it, like he wasn't sure how I'd react.

"Seriously?"

Shrugging, he looked down at the dirt. "They fight all the time. I didn't even tell them about Parents' Day. They just would have made a scene, like they did last year."

I sighed. "Sorry," I said.

Peter looked up at me. Half of his mouth ticked up in a weak smile. "It's okay."

I nodded, getting him completely. "Not really," I said.

"Not really," he agreed. Peter took another sip of his smoothie, and I realized that this was the longest conversation I'd ever had with him. He was my

Cinderella—the handsome guy I liked, even though I didn't really know him at all. I wished I'd spent less time swooning over him, and a little more time talking to him. We could have been friends. Maybe if I moved to Houston, we would be.

"Hey, Pete!" Shaz shouted, waving frantically. "Pete! Get over here!"

Peter nodded at him, then turned to me. "Guess I'd better go. See you at the games lawn?"

"See you," I said.

chapter thirteen

"*T*hose look great." Greta waved at the cluster of balloons I had taped to the windowsill. "Like a giant flower. This was a brilliant idea!"

"I'm a natural genius," I told her.

"It runs in the family," she shot back, and I laughed.

"Yoo-hoo!" Aunt Kate's voice called from the front hall. "Girls! We're back!"

"Just a sec!" I shouted.

"That was fast!" Greta hurried to plump up the pillows while I taped the last balloon in place.

A moment later, the door swung open, and Uncle Dave pushed Grandma's wheelchair into the room.

"Hey!" My uncle smiled hugely as his eyes traced

over the red and yellow crepe-paper streamers we had hung in a spiraling pinwheel from the light at the center of the ceiling. "It looks great in here!"

"It was Mieka's idea," Greta said quickly. "I just helped."

"Welcome back, Grandma." My voice was shy—I sounded about six years old.

"Thank you, Mieka." Grandma's lips were set in a line, and she still looked tired. Still, it was the nicest thing she had ever said to me—at least, that I could remember—and it felt like a victory.

"Balloons!" Mark cried as he burst into the room. He punched the red one, and it slammed back against the window and bounced forward again, like a punching bag.

"Do you think you could control your children?" Grandma snapped at Aunt Kate.

"Mark, honey, come over here with me," my aunt said. Reluctantly, Mark left the balloons and stomped over to stand by his mother.

Dad and Uncle Dave grunted as they heaved Grandma onto the bed. Dad had said that it was lucky she didn't need a hospital bed, but I wondered as I watched him struggle to help her up. I could understand wanting to be in your own bed . . . but I couldn't imagine having to work so hard to get into it. Grandma was fully dressed in a pink sweat suit, and she was carrying her purse, which she refused to set down as she collapsed onto her back.

Aunt Kate stuck a pillow behind Grandma's head, and she settled back against it. With a snap, she clicked open her purse and took out a pack of cigarettes.

"Mom, what do you think you're doing?" Dad cried as Aunt Kate lunged for the pack. But Grandma held on to them with an iron claw, half crumpling the pack as my aunt tried to grab them away.

"Get off!" Grandma shouted.

"Hand them over!" Aunt Kate commanded, not letting go.

Grandma batted her over the head with her pocketbook. "You don't get to tell me what to do!"

"Okay, Kate, okay," Uncle Dave said, taking his wife by the arm. She tried to shake him off, but he held firm. "Your mama can decide on her own," he said in a low voice.

"Thank you, David," Grandma said stiffly. "I'm glad

someone around here knows how to respect their elders." She pulled a bent menthol from the pack, straightened it a little, and lit the end, inhaling deeply. With a hacking cough, she lay back against the pillows and looked out at us. "Well, ain't this a pitcher," she said. I thought she meant something about how we were like a big jug, about to pour love all over her, but then I got it. She meant *picture*.

"Mom, Mieka has something for you," my dad said, touching my elbow gently.

I pulled the small package wrapped in bright silver paper off the windowsill. In my house, we usually just wrap gifts in newspaper, but Aunt Kate has a whole closet dedicated to wrapping paper and ribbons and tape and boxes and bags and tissue paper, so I'd been able to wrap it perfectly, with a red ribbon on top, just like in a magazine. I handed the box to Grandma, who lifted one eyebrow.

"Well, I certainly am gettin' spoiled today," Grandma said drily. "You folks must think I'm on my deathbed." She held the cigarette in one hand and stabbed the paper with a long fingernail on the other, tearing it along the edge. Pulling the box open, she pulled out a wad of tissue paper, uncovering the bowl. She looked at it like she wasn't a hundred percent sure what it was, then held it up.

"Mieka made it for you," Dad said. "At camp."

A warm glow spread through me. It was pride, I think, and happiness, too. Maybe Grandma and I can be friends, after all, I thought. Maybe we can be a normal family. . . .

Greta beamed.

"How nice," Grandma said. Then she flicked the ash from her cigarette into the bowl.

I felt the seconds buzz by, as loud as horseflies, as I stood there—still as a stone. The room was so quiet that the bowl made a clear clink, clunk as Grandma set my little sea anemone on the bedside table and took another puff from her cigarette.

"Mother," my dad said in a low voice, "what . . . ?" He couldn't even finish his sentence, just shook his head.

"What?" Grandma puffed up, like a cobra. "It's an ashtray, isn't it?"

"Of course it's not an ashtray, Mother!" my dad cried. "Do you seriously think that Mieka would make you an ashtray?" He didn't sound angry, exactly—he sounded more like he couldn't believe what he'd just seen.

"Well, I don't see what the big deal is," Uncle Dave said.

"Of course you don't," Aunt Kate snapped.

Grandma pursed her lips into a frown. "I can use it however I want to."

"That's the *point*, Mother." Dad's voice was heavy—I'd never heard him be sarcastic before, and it sounded strange. "That is so like you—you don't even care that your granddaughter made this for you. You just care about what you want."

The minute—the second—that those words floated past his lips, Grandma picked up "the ashtray" and hurled it against the wall. It just missed a framed picture of Aunt Kate and Greta smiling on the deck of a boat, and hit the paint, leaving a brown mark against the smooth yellow. As it dropped, the ash spilled out, trickling a gray stain onto the ivory carpet. I stared down at the pieces of my sea anemone. There were seven of them.

"You care more about a stupid bowl than about your own mother," Grandma snarled, but I'm not sure if my dad even heard her. He was staring at the bowl, too. So was Greta. We all were. Everyone except for Grandma, who glared out the window, puffed on her cigarette, and ashed onto the floor.

Feeling like I was in a dream, I walked over to where the pieces of my sea anemone lay scattered. Nobody spoke as I picked them up, one by one, but Grandma gave me a look, like she was disgusted with me.

It was the look, more than anything else, that got me. I couldn't stop myself. "Why are you so mean?" I asked her.

She opened her mouth in a tiny circle, like a fish, but no words came out. It's not like I was expecting an answer, anyway. I was already walking out the door, my broken bowl cradled in my hands.

The pool shimmered softly in the late afternoon air, while all around me strange insects whirred their deafening alarm. A trickle of sweat threaded its way down my spine. Hot air hung over me, damp as a cloud. I splashed my feet into the clear blue water, but it didn't help much. Just made the rest of me feel hotter.

Why do things always break into triangles? I

wondered as I looked down at the brown pieces in my hands. The part that had been glazed was dark brown, but the cracks had exposed the clay underneath, which was almost red. It hadn't seemed red while I was making it. I wondered if something about the kiln had changed the color—all of that baking. So much baking that it changed you on the inside. The way my skin had changed color over the weeks I was here, so that I looked like a slice of bread popped up from the toaster.

I set the pieces of my bowl down by the side of the pool, and held two of them against each other. They fit. I could fix it, I thought. The cracks were so clean, they would hardly show once they were glued back together. I would know they were there, of course, but maybe nobody else would.

"Hey." My dad's voice was soft behind me, but I didn't turn to face him.

"I'm not going to say I'm sorry," I told him. "I'm not sorry." Beneath the glassy water, fine bubbles clung to my legs, like tiny diamonds.

"No," Dad said. "I guess you're not." I heard him rip off his Velcro sandals, and then his legs sighed into the pool beside mine. "I'm not sorry, either," he added after a moment.

I looked up into his face. A warm breeze caught his silvery hair, sending it rippling like grain. He squinted at the sky, deepening the laugh lines at the edges of his eyes. It occurred to me that I couldn't remember the last time I'd seen my father laugh. At home, he laughed all of the time. He cracked himself up over lines from movies, or silly signs by the side of the road, or jingles on the radio. When he was in the right mood, I could say almost anything, and it would put him into a fit. But he didn't laugh here.

He looked down at the seven pieces of my bowl, laid out beside my hand. The pieces curled up, like fingers. "Are you going to fix it?"

"I think so," I told him. I touched one pointy tip gently, and it rocked toward me on its curved back. "But I'm not giving it to *her* again."

"I wouldn't, either."

At the edge of the sky, the clouds glowed pink, lit by the fading light. In the distance, a church steeple glowed with the same faint color, the same as the inside of a shell.

"Your grandmother's a very unhappy person, Mieka," Dad started.

"I know." I had tried so hard to understand what it was like to be old and sick and lonely. But that didn't always make it easier to deal with Grandma.

"But I don't think that should be your problem." My father mashed his lips together, like he didn't want to finish his thought. Finally, it came sighing out of him. "And I don't think it should be mine, either."

My chest sank. "The Bible says that you should forgive people."

Dad's long fingers traced across the stubble on his jaw. "It also says that you should obey your parents, as I recall."

I nodded. The fifth commandment, as I had recently learned. "It does." I thought for a moment. "Dad," I asked, "why do you hate religion?"

His lips pursed slightly in surprise. "I don't hate religion," he said after a moment.

"You don't go to church," I said to him. "And you didn't want me to go to Camp Franklin."

Dad drew in a deep breath, and then let it all out at once, like he was letting his chest deflate. "When your mother and I got married . . ." he said slowly, then he stopped and looked at me carefully, like he was wondering if I really wanted to know.

"What happened?" I asked.

Dad looked down at the sparkling water. "Your mom was raised Jewish, and I was raised Episcopalian," Dad said. "And when we announced that we were getting married, Grandma refused to come."

"What?" My voice felt strangled in my throat.

"She said that it wasn't right to marry outside of your religion." He picked up one of the sharp pieces of my bowl, tracing a finger along one edge. "And after that, I never felt right about religion. Anyone's."

"She's so mean," I said.

"She wasn't always." Dad sighed. "But when Dad— your grandfather—died, she changed." He turned to look at me. "You don't have to go to church to be a good person, Mieka," Dad said.

"I know," I said. I thought about Camp Franklin, and Pastor Mike, and Jewel. "But sometimes it helps you remember to try."

My dad covered his mouth with his fingers, the way he does when he's thinking. "Well," he said after a moment, "maybe we could go to church sometimes. If you really want to." There was a long pause. Finally, Dad heaved a heavy sigh. "Mieka," he said, "I've decided not to take the job."

"Good." I kicked, sending a splash halfway across the pool.

"Really?"

"I never wanted you to take the job, anyway," I said. "You're an artist, Dad. You can't just become something else."

"How did you get to be so smart?" Reaching out, he tucked a piece of my frizzy hair behind my ear.

"Genetics."

Dad laughed then. A real laugh, like he was reaching down past his belly to his toes for it. That laugh was contagious—it made me giggle.

"I doubt that," he said finally.

"No? Must be that fancy public school, then."

"Worth every penny," Dad agreed.

Around me, the crazy insects whirred and whirred, and then stopped. Even in the sudden silence, my head rang with their song. "Why can't we be normal?" I asked.

My dad's dark eyebrows disappeared beneath his silver hair. "What do you mean?"

I shrugged. I wasn't even sure *what* I meant. "I mean—like Aunt Kate and Uncle Dave. Or like Greta."

Dad's smile lines danced and his deep brown eyes sparkled. He was laughing. Quietly, though. "What's so normal about them?"

"Well—" I started to explain that Aunt Kate was nice all of the time and Uncle Dave had a real job and Greta was pretty and everyone liked her and that Mark was a genius . . . but then I thought about it, and stopped. Aunt Kate was nice, sure—too nice. It made her mad at the wrong people sometimes. And Uncle Dave made a lot of money—but he was never around. And Greta—well, she wasn't even sure who her real friends were. She couldn't even tell them the truth. Even Mark had problems. "Forget it," I said finally.

"There's no such thing as normal," Dad said. Wrapping his arm around me, he pulled me into a hug.

"Yeah," I agreed. "Yeah, tell me about it."

chapter fourteen

"Aren't you going to have breakfast?" Greta asked as I slowly folded my yellow dress and packed it carefully at the top of my bag.

"They'll give us something on the plane," I told her. "But you should go down. I'm almost done."

"I'll wait," Greta said, sitting on her neat purple bed-spread.

"I might be a few minutes," I told her. "I want to check around—make sure I've got everything. I don't want to leave my toothbrush in the bathroom, or anything."

Greta stood up. "Are you sure?"

I nodded. "I'll be there in a sec."

Finally, finally, she left. Wow, that girl cannot take a hint, I thought as I pulled the bundled up T-shirt out of my bag and unwrapped the bowl. Dad had helped me glue it back together. You could still see the cracks where it had shattered, but it didn't look bad. The seams are the Persian Flaw, I thought. In a way, the bowl wouldn't have been complete without them.

I set the bowl on Greta's bedside table. I'd already placed a note inside.

"Mieka, we've got to get going." Dad was standing in the doorway to Greta's room. Her lavender walls reflected on his skin, making him look rosy. Or maybe he was just excited to be heading home. I know I was— even though I was sad to leave, too.

"I'm almost ready," I told him. I zipped up my bag and slung the strap over my shoulder, and then there was only one thing left to do.

"Come on," Dad said, taking my hand. "We've got to say good-bye to Grandma."

Nodding, I followed him. The television was blaring so loud I could hear it halfway down the hall. Grandma didn't turn it off when we walked into her room, although she did turn down the volume a little.

"Mom," Dad said, standing at the foot of her bed, "Mieka and I are about to leave for the airport."

"Airport?" Her eyes snapped onto my father's. I think it was the first time in the entire trip that he had her full attention. "You just got here."

"We stayed three weeks," Dad said. "I've got to get back."

"Why?" Grandma asked, practically sneering. "It's not like you have to get back to the office."

Dad closed his eyes for a moment, as though he was letting her words float past. I counted to twelve before he opened them again. "We came to say good-bye," he said.

"You barely even said hello," Grandma told us.

I swallowed hard, and said the line I'd been practicing all night before I went to bed. "I love you, Grandma," I told her.

"That's what you *say* . . ." Grandma said. She left the sentence unfinished, and that was that. Not exactly heartwarming. But I'd tried. One last time, I'd tried to be good.

"Take care of yourself, Mom," my father said.

"I'm the only one who will," Grandma Baker said. Then she turned the television up. Loud.

My father touched my shoulder and guided me out of the room.

"All right, everybody ready?" Uncle Dave asked as he strode down the hall. "I think we've got all of the luggage in the back. Dang, you people travel light. You should see us—we need six suitcases just for Greta!" His laughed boomed as he patted my dad on the back.

"Do you have everything?" Dad asked me.

I thought about the bowl on Greta's bedside table. "Everything I'm taking with me," I told him.

"What am I going to do?" Greta wailed as she buried her face into my shoulder. Her tears had already soaked the other sleeve, turning my arm chilly in the frigid over-air-conditioned airport.

"I can come back for a visit," I said. "Or you can come and visit me."

I regretted saying it the minute the words were out of my mouth. What would Greta think of our tiny little apartment? Of the mess?

"Can I?" Her head shot off my shoulder and her blue eyes sparkled eagerly. "Oh, can I? Mom, can I go visit

Mieka and Uncle Jeff? Can I go with them right now?" Greta grabbed my hand and squeezed it as hard as I squeeze the nurse's hand when I'm getting a shot. I smiled, even though my fingers were being crushed.

Greta was young—younger than I was, even though we were the same age. But she was sweet. And she liked me, even though I didn't always deserve it.

"You can't go now," Aunt Kate said reasonably. "You don't have a ticket."

"Maybe at Thanksgiving?" I suggested. "Or over Christmas break? You could see snow," I told Greta, who gasped, as though I had promised her a land filled with fairies.

"I want to go, too!" Mark cried.

"You're not old enough," Greta told him.

"Yes I am. I am too old enough," Mark insisted.

Thankfully, a voice ended this argument when it announced that our plane was now boarding. Dad glanced at the long line that wound around the security checkpoint. It was full of people who looked bored, or impatient, or impatient and bored. They all had carry-on bags. A compact little man with a head like a magic eight ball kicked his small red duffel forward, while a sweaty overweight woman in turquoise leggings lugged a tan bag on wheels. Dad and I didn't have any bags—we'd already checked them in at the curb. We'd had three—one more than when I arrived, one that was full of the clothes that Aunt Kate had bought me.

My dad extended his hand to Uncle Dave. "Dave," he said, "thanks so much for everything."

"I'm sorry we couldn't get you to stay," my uncle said, and he really sounded like he meant it.

A quick purse of the lips and a nod told me that my dad was weighing his words. "I think I'm doing what's best for Mieka," he said at last.

Uncle Dave's eyebrow shot up—just one—in a look that said "I doubt that," but I knew what my father meant. And he was right. He was doing what was best for both of us, even though it wasn't easy.

Dad wrapped Aunt Kate in a huge hug and whispered something into her hair. I couldn't hear what he said, but she nodded a few times and hugged him hard. "I will," she promised.

Mark wrapped his arms around my waist. "I'll miss you," he said.

"Me, too, squirt," I told him.

"I'm not a squirt," he said, but he was smiling.

Then Greta threw her arms around me and tried to choke me to death, or at least that was what it felt like. "Don't forget me," she whispered.

"I won't."

"No." Greta backed away a little so that she could look me in the eye. "I mean it." She was telling me not to forget the *real* her.

"I couldn't," I told her, and it was the truth.

Dad and I moved into place behind the sweaty woman and her tan bag, and the Willistons waved, then turned and trudged off. I was glad that they weren't going to stand there while we went through the security line. That always makes me feel like I'm on display, and I wind up making faces and acting silly, when really all I want is to be alone with the sad, hollow feeling I have at leaving someone behind.

"I'm glad we left Grandma at home," I said.

"She hates airports." Dad's voice was automatic, like he wasn't even thinking about what he was saying. We kicked off our shoes and put them on the belt, too, then we both passed through the metal detector. It didn't beep, so I guess we weren't a threat to anybody.

The plane was almost finished boarding by the time we got to the gate, so we didn't have to wait in line before we handed our tickets to the beautiful woman at the counter. With her plum-colored glossy lips and her hair tucked into a perfect bun and her crisp navy uniform, she looked like a fashion doll. The kind that you see dressed as a doctor or a movie star or president of the United States. Today she was a flight attendant doll.

"Have a great flight," she said, and winked at me. It was the wink more than anything that reminded me she wasn't just a doll, after all. Like Greta. Like Peter.

"Thanks," I said to her, and followed my father into the long, gray tunnel of the Jetway.

Dad looked down at the tickets, checking our seats, then turned to me. "Are you ready to go home?"

"Yes," I told him. "I'm ready."